CATHERINE O'FLYNN

LORI
and
MAX

AND THE
BOOK THIEVES

Firefly

First published in 2020
by Firefly Press
25 Gabalfa Road, Llandaff North, Cardiff, CF14 2JJ
www.fireflypress.co.uk

A CIP catalogue record of this book is available
from the British Library.

ISBN 9781913102357

This book has been published with the support of
the Welsh Books Council.

Typeset by Elaine Sharples

Printed by CPI Group UK

CHAPTER ONE

It's a typical Thursday afternoon at New Heath Primary School. Rain streams down the outside of the windows, the radiators are on full blast and I'm carrying out routine surveillance on my classmates. I sneak my top-secret notebook out of my pocket and look around discreetly. Class 6B is supposed to be doing silent reading, but even someone without my advanced level observation skills could see that pretty much nobody in the room is either silent or reading.

Jessica Pemberton and Maryam Begum are playing Rock Paper Scissors. Mustafa P. is writing AVFC on his knuckles with a Sharpie. Rosy Hannah is drawing a picture of a guinea pig (unless I tell you otherwise assume Rosy Hannah is always drawing a picture of a guinea pig because … well … she always is) and Kelly Keogh has nodded off.

I pick up my pencil and write the day's date in my notebook. I take another long look around the room, sigh and write in small letters:

Nothing to report

Everyone in 6B knows that 'silent reading' is just code. Not the kind of exciting top-secret code used by undercover detectives, but the kind of really quite boring and sometimes confusing code used by teachers. When Mr Probert says, 'Take out your books and get on with some silent reading', what he really means is, 'Give me five minutes to get the interactive whiteboard working again.' Everyone knows this.

Everyone that is except Max Ellington who sits next to me and is actually silent and is actually reading. Max is the tallest person in the class and seems even taller as, no matter how hard she tries (and to be honest I'm not sure she tries that hard), her hair always sticks straight up.

Max is currently buried in a book called *Marsupial Factfile* and nothing will distract her. I reckon that Max already knows more facts about marsupials and probably every other species and sub-species of animal on earth than most people would think normal. Max isn't what most people would think normal though, she'd be the first to say that.

Community Learning & Libraries
Cymuned Ddysgu a Llyfrgelloedd

Newport
CITY COUNCIL
CYNGOR DINAS
Casnewydd

This item should be returned or renewed by the
last date stamped below.

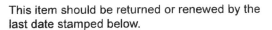

Library

-------------------	-------------------	-------------------
-------------------	-------------------	-------------------
-------------------	-------------------	-------------------
-------------------	-------------------	-------------------
-------------------	-------------------	-------------------
-------------------	-------------------	-------------------
-------------------	-------------------	-------------------
-------------------	-------------------	-------------------
-------------------	-------------------	-------------------
-------------------	-------------------	-------------------

To renew visit:

www.newport.gov.uk/libraries

Catherine O'Flynn grew up in a sweetshop. She's the author of three novels for grown-ups including the Costa First Novel Award-winning *What Was Lost*. Her first book featuring Lori and Max was long-listed for the 2020 Branford Boase Award and the Blue Peter Awards 2020. Catherine is a former child detective who failed ever to solve a crime.

For Dory, Edie and Peter –
my bubble entire.

As I've mentioned, I spend my 'silent reading' time scanning the room for clues, suspects or any hint of criminal intent. Some people would say that keeping a constant eye on my classmates and noting down details about them in a secret notebook isn't what most people would think normal either. That's probably why Max and I stick together.

I'm Lori Mason and I'm a private detective. Or at least I would be if I had anything to detect. I had a big break earlier in the year when I cracked a major case. Max went missing, cash was stolen and the class hamster was involved in money laundering. Since then though things have been quiet. Too quiet. There was the short-lived mystery of Elijah Stephen's missing bike last month, but it turned out Mr Cheetham the caretaker had just moved it because it was a trip hazard. (If Mr Cheetham was a superhero, Trip Hazard would be the name of his arch-enemy. His life is an endless, one-man battle against things left lying on the ground.) I mean, I was glad for Elijah that the bike turned up, but if I'm completely honest I was also a bit disappointed. I wanted mystery, intrigue, deception and cover-up, not another one of Mr Cheetham's really quite long PowerPoint presentations on health and safety. It's not that I long for bad things to happen but crime-fighting is tough when there's just no crime.

The only remotely interesting recent developments are that a new boy has joined the class this term and so has a new teacher. The new boy is called Taylor Barclay and he's quite small and very skinny. The new teacher is called Mr Probert and he's quite tall and very shiny. Miss Casey used to be our teacher. She was extremely forgetful, especially with names and she lost things almost as often as my nan does (about eighty per cent – or four fifths – of my nan's time is spent looking for either her glasses, her purse or her keys). But even though Miss Casey spent two terms calling me Lisa rather than Lori and calling everyone else, including the girls, Colin (note: there isn't a single Colin in the school), I thought she was a good teacher. Now she's off having a baby and I have dedicated a page in my secret notebook to my concerns regarding this.

Pros and Cons of Miss Casey becoming a parent:

Pro:

1. *Miss Casey seemed really happy when she made the announcement. (Not entirely sure if happiness was due to impending baby or impending long break from Class 6B).*

Cons:

1. *Miss Casey just cannot remember names. Will this be any better with her own child? Or will Baby Casey grow up unsure if it is actually called Colin or not?*

Proposed solution: Miss Casey should probably call the baby – boy or girl – Colin just to be on safe side.

2. *Miss Casey can't remember where she's put things. Will this be any better with her own child? Or will little Colin be left in a toilet/on the photocopier/ in the boot of her car/ in any of the other places Miss Casey regularly loses things?*

Proposed solution: attach little Colin to Magic-Find-That-Key keyring, like the one I got Nan last Christmas. When you lose your keys/baby/similar, you just whistle and the Magic-Find-That-Key keyring emits electronic bleeps. (This hasn't been so useful for Nan as it turns out she can't whistle and neither can I. In fact, both the Magic-Find-That-Key keyring and attached keys to our house were lost by Boxing Day. Note to self: check if Miss Casey can whistle.)

3. *While Miss Casey is on maternity leave, we're left with Mr Probert.*

Mr Probert is nothing like Miss Casey. He never forgets our names or loses anything. He wears smart suits, drives a big shiny car and uses an LED pointer. If we get a question right Mr Probert has an alarming habit of shouting 'Boom!' loudly. I've actually stopped putting my hand up to answer questions as a direct result. Mr Probert is an NQT which means Newly Qualified Teacher but before he became a teacher he worked in 'business' for fifteen years. He talks about *business* a lot but he never actually says what business he was in. I find this quite mysterious. He's told us (several times) about the fateful day he realised he needed to share all he'd learnt from *business* with the next generation and decided to become a teacher. Mr Probert is always talking about the 'real world'. When Harry Besley copied Yasmin Oldershaw's work, Mr Probert said, 'you wouldn't get away with that in the real world'; if we are slow lining up for lunch he says 'this won't cut the mustard in the real world!' I don't know if I'm the only person who finds this confusing and worrying. What is this if it's not the real world?

The other big change this term is that we no longer have school on Friday afternoons. Mr Wilson the headteacher has been saying for years that the school hasn't got any money. That's why the trim trail in the playground was never replaced after the wood rotted and it fell apart. And why part of the hall has been taped off for ages due to water damage. And why Mr Cheetham handed out cards not presents when he dressed up as Father Christmas last year. 'We've tightened our belts as much as we can,' said Mr Wilson in a special assembly, 'but I'm sad to say it hasn't been enough. The terrible truth is that we can no longer afford to open on Friday afternoons.' He said that by closing early the school will save a bit of money on staffing and can start to repay its debts. I don't understand how the school owes money or to who or for what. I thought about asking Mr Probert but I was sure the answer would involve the 'real world', so I decided not to.

Everyone is shocked and outraged. There have been lots of protests about the government cuts, our school has even been on the *News at Ten*! Max and I walked home together a few days after the announcement. 'It's not fair,' said Max. 'It means we get less education than other kids.'

'I know,' I said. 'Nan says it's a scandal. She says it will be very harmful for us in the long term.'

'I mean three hours a week, that's 30 hours less a term, that's … 90 hours less a school year.' Max added it all up in her head. She's very good at maths. 'That's like us having an extra three weeks of holiday compared to everyone else!'

'I know,' I said, though I hadn't actually realised that until she said it. 'It's just really, really…' We looked at each other 'Good!' said Max.

'Amazing!' I agreed and we laughed and laughed all the way home.

CHAPTER TWO

Max is in her flat. She is trying to read Fang's mind. She lies on the living-room floor staring into his eyes. Fang is Max's guard dog. The worst thing that ever happened to Max is that she was abducted for a few days and everyone except Lori thought she'd run away. The best thing that ever happened was that her mum let her get a rescue dog after she'd been found safe. Some people might think that Fang is maybe on the small side for a guard dog, but Max is sure he's tough enough for the job. His fur is a mixture of black, white and grey and always sticks up, a bit like Max's hair. His eyes are brown, but one is much paler than the other. He sleeps at the foot of Max's bed every night. When Max has a bad dream she stretches her legs down until her toes touch Fang and she can feel him breathing in and out. She tries to imagine what dreams he has. She hopes they're always happy.

A key turns in the door and Max's mum,

Angela, calls 'Hello!' She sheds her coat and bags before coming in and sitting down heavily on the sofa.

'What a day,' she says and closes her eyes. Fang trots over and licks her hand.

'Hello boy,' she says.

'You're late, Mum,' says Max, getting up.

'I'm sorry. Aisha was off sick so I had to stay on for an hour and then that turned into two.'

Max touches her mum's cheek. 'You're cold.'

'I know, heating's still broken. You never get warm in that place, even though you're running about all day.'

'You need another job, Mum. A better job.'

Angela smiles. 'Who's going to give me a better job?'

'Lots of people. There's all kinds of things you could do.'

'Maxie, do you know how many qualifications I have?'

Max shrugs. 'I know you didn't do so well at school…'

'Zero. Not a single one.'

'Doesn't mean you're not clever.'

'Maybe not. It means I don't get a better job

though. Long hours, low pay – that's what I do. I shouldn't complain. It's better than doing nothing. I need this job. Idleness isn't good for me, but let me be a lesson to you: work hard at school, then you can be what you like.'

'I'm going to be a zoologist.'

'Are they rich?'

Max shrugs again. 'I don't know.'

Angela looks horrified. 'What?! You need to know! Don't pick a job that pays bad, Maxie. Whatever you do, be rich! Life's a lot easier if you are.'

Max smiles. 'OK, I promise I'll be rich enough to take care of you and Fang.'

'OK, it's a deal.' Angela stretches her legs out in front of her. 'I need a hot drink.'

'I'll make you one.'

'No, wait, tell me about your day first. How was school?'

Max tries to remember her day. 'School was OK, I think. Just normal. We had a maths test which was easy. Lori brought in the new *Paperclips* catalogue.'

'The what catalogue?'

'*Paperclips*, you know, the shop.'

'Oh – yeah I think so, sells office stuff.'

'Yeah. Lori loves that stuff. *Paperclips* is her favourite shop. New catalogue has just come out, so she was busy looking through that all lunchtime.'

'OK,' her mum says uncertainly. 'And what do you do while she's looking at pictures of pens?'

'I was reading about marmosets.'

'Oh boy, you two know how to have a good time! What happened to playing kiss chase in the playground?'

'Mum!'

Her mum laughs. 'You see! That's how I ended up with no qualifications. Stick to marmosets. What have you been doing since you got in?'

'Brain-training Fang.'

'Oh, my poor boy.' Angela reaches out and strokes Fang. 'Has she been making you learn about marmosets too?' She glances at Max. 'Still don't know why you called him Fang. He's just not a Fang type of dog. I'd have gone for Mr Cuddles or Poochie or Sir Snuffalot.'

Max looks unimpressed. 'I know Mum, that's why I named him. He's a dog, a guard dog, not a fluffy toy.'

Her mum ruffles the fur on Fang's head. 'Don't listen to her, boy. I think you're very cute.'

'Mum, he's a highly intelligent animal.'

Angela frowns. 'Cute yes, but intelligent … are you sure? I see you throwing those sticks for him – he never brings them back.'

'That's what proves his intelligence! Why would I want him bringing me things I've thrown away? That would make him a dumb dog.'

Her mum seems doubtful but shrugs. 'Maybe, Max. You're the expert. You've certainly read enough books about it anyway.'

Max goes and makes some tea. When she comes back Angela pats the sofa next to her.

'I spoke to your dad on the phone on the way home.'

Max's mum and dad separated earlier in the year. They got along OK most of the time, but her dad had some problems with gambling. After Max's abduction he decided life would be more settled for her if he moved away.

'What did he say?'

'He's up north somewhere. Blackburn, was it? Burnley? Blackpool? I can't remember – something like that.'

'Did he sound OK?'

'Yeah. He's OK, I think.' She pauses. 'Well, you know what your dad's like. He wouldn't want you worrying about him anyway.'

'Will we see him soon?'

Angela sighs. 'I don't know really. You can ask him yourself – he's going to ring you later. Talking of which, look I've got something for you.' She reaches in her back pocket and pulls out her phone. Max waits for her to do something with it, but she just holds it out. Max shrugs. 'What? It's your phone.'

'No. It was my phone. Now it's yours.'

Max frowns as her mum puts it in her hand.

'I don't like you being at home on your own and I can't reach you. I worry about you when I'm late at work and now on Friday afternoons when you're not at school. I got a better deal, new contract, new phone, same tariff. This one's yours now. It's not the latest model – you know that, but it's OK. You can video, it's got internet – all that.'

Max looks at the phone. Now they're old enough to walk home from school on their own lots of people in her class have phones. Some people have the latest smart phones, others have battered old cast offs. Even Lori has one, though hers is a bit weird. Her nan bought it and the shop assistant must have thought the phone was for Nan herself because it's a special model for elderly people. It has giant buttons to make dialling and texting easier and an emergency contact function in case urgent assistance is ever required. Lori never uses it.

'But what about the money? How will you afford it?' says Max.

'I can manage, just don't be making loads of calls. It's pay-as-you-go. Use it when it's important and we shouldn't have to top it up too often.'

Max nods. 'I'll be careful, Mum. I'll try and use stuff that doesn't cost anything. Like the camera – hey, I can make videos of Fang!' She stands up. 'Come on, boy, let's do some drills and then I'll video you.'

At that moment a phone starts ringing. It's an unfamiliar ringtone. Max looks at the phone in her hand, but her mum reaches for her handbag:

'Ooh, that's my new phone.' She fishes it out and holds it up for Max to see.

'Nice, isn't it?'

'Answer it!' says Max. Her mum pulls a face at her and then takes the call.

While Angela speaks on the phone Max starts preparing a mini-agility course for Fang. She constructs barriers from cushions and a tunnel from two chairs. Fang lies on the sofa watching all this with little apparent interest in moving. Max is particularly pleased with a ramp she constructs from a tray leaning on a cereal box.

'Come on, Fang! It's ready. Let's show Mum what you can do.' But Fang is distracted, his eyes are on Angela and his head is cocked as if he's listening to the phone call. 'Hey!' calls Max. 'Come on, boy. Remember you need to focus.' But as Angela finishes the call, Fang jumps up on her lap and licks her hand. It's only now that Max notices her mum looks upset.

'What is it?'

'That was the letting agency.'

'Who?'

'The people we rent the flat from. They said the landlord wants to sell. He's got a buyer lined up.'

'Sell what? A buyer for what?'

Max's mum takes a deep breath. 'Here, Maxie, our home. We need to find somewhere new to live.'

CHAPTER THREE

We are studying local history at school. There's a big map of New Heath stuck on the back wall and we've all marked our houses on it with coloured pins. We've been researching what New Heath was like at the beginning of the twentieth century. Mr Probert seems really into local history. I wonder if this might be a clue as to what 'business' he used to work in. I discreetly open my secret notebook at the relevant page:

Mr Probert's Former Business – facts and theories
Fact: subject has a very shiny car
Fact: subject wears very shiny shoes
Theory: something related to polish? Maybe Mr Probert invented a particularly effective hybrid shoe/car polish.
Note: check if a product called 'Probert's Polish' (or similar) exists.

I add my new fact:

Fact: keen interest in New Heath and its history
Theory: maybe Probert's business HQ is/was in New
Heath.
Note: research businesses on New Heath High Street:
Select n Save, Tanning Shop, Rooster Party, Ritzy
Fashions, Vape-o-rama, Supercigs etc etc. Maybe
show photo of Probert while questioning employees?

This morning we're looking at a map from 1889 projected onto the board. We're working our way around the class trying to identify where everyone lives now. Mr Probert says there are signs of the past all around us and all we have to do is keep our eyes open and look out for them. He says we need to take the time to be more observant and pick up on clues. I grit my teeth. It's at times like this that I have this mad urge to take my top-secret notebook (which of course Mr Probert has never even noticed me carrying, because that's how observant he actually is), opening it at any random page filled with my observations and close surveillance notes, slapping it on his desk and shouting, 'Is this observant enough for you?' Obviously, I don't though. One – because I'm not really a shouting-at-teachers kind of person. I find any kind of shouting or telling off a bit stressful. Two – because I'm undercover and nobody ever said that was easy. One day though when I'm a world-famous detective I guess Mr Probert is going to look back and feel a bit foolish.

Anyway, it turns out that the map is actually very interesting. Max's flat stands right in the middle of what used to be a farm, which makes her happy as now she can imagine animals roaming around her kitchen and bedroom; Mustafa P's house used to be some kind of tavern, and Grace Montero's block of maisonettes used to be in the grounds of a big posh house. My house is a bit disappointing as it turns out it hasn't changed – same house then as now, different people though obviously. I close my eyes and try and picture someone living in our house in Victorian times. I imagine a pipe and then a hat and then a magnifying glass and then I realise I'm thinking of Sherlock Holmes again. It happens a lot.

'What about you, Taylor,' says Mr Probert to the new boy. 'Where do you live?' Taylor's not that new now. He's been here for half a term, but I think I've only heard him speak once. His cheeks turn red as he answers in a quiet voice.

'The Glebe, sir.'

'Ah right, the Glebe estate. Well, that's definitely going to have changed since 1919 as that whole estate is only about forty or fifty years old. Whereabouts on the Glebe do you live?'

Taylor answers but his voice is now even quieter and impossible for human ears to pick up.

'Speak up a bit, Taylor,' says Mr Probert.

'Norcross Tower, sir.' But now Taylor's turned his volume up too loud and it comes out as a shout and some of the class laugh.

'Right,' says Mr Probert, moving the cursor on the projected map. 'That's on Devon Close, isn't it? Let's have a look. Devon Close didn't even exist a hundred years ago. Look – that whole area was actually … a quarry. Now that is interesting.' He turns to look at us and check we're all paying attention. 'Back in Victorian times there weren't any bin lorries or bin men who came and took your rubbish and recycling away. People had to dispose of their own refuse – often taking it in a cart or barrow of some kind – and interestingly these quarries were often where people would dump their rubbish.'

'Nothing's changed there then, the Glebe's still a total dump!' shouts out Tyrone Baldwin. More people laugh but Mr Probert is angry and sends Tyrone straight out of the class. He sets us some work and then goes over to speak to Taylor quietly.

I turn to Max and whisper, 'I'll have to tell Nan there used to be a dump out at the Glebe.'

Max carries on sketching a map. 'Why?'

'She can go on one of her treasure hunts.'

'What treasure is she going to find in an old rubbish dump?'

'Well, Victorian bottles and jars for a start – rare ones can be valuable. Some go for hundreds of pounds.'

Max stops drawing and looks at me. 'How do you know?'

'Don't you watch *Treasure Hunters*? It's on the Leisure Quest Channel about eight times a day.'

Nan loves *Treasure Hunters* so much that it's started to take over her life. Nan used to have two hobbies – collecting ceramic angels and wearing crazy hats. To be honest, if she was going to lose a hobby, I personally would have opted for the crazy hat wearing, as its really difficult to keep a low profile and remain undercover when you're in the company of Nan in one of her hats (particularly on her sombrero days). But she still loves the hats and it's the ceramic angel passion that's faded or at least she's run out of any more to buy for now. Her new obsession is finding valuable antiques, just like Hugo Smythe does on *Treasure Hunters*.

If you've never watched *Treasure Hunters*, it's basically a programme about a man in a hat (another reason why Nan loves him) digging around in old barns, factories and other dirty, damp buildings and getting very excited when he finds dirty, damp and often broken chairs or statues or bits of old signs. He buys this rubbish cheap, cleans it up a bit and puts it in his shop. Then – and this is the bit that baffles me – lots of rich and/or mad people pay hundreds and hundreds of pounds for that same rubbish. Every time Hugo buys or sells anything he shakes the other person's hand very vigorously and says, 'Now that's a lovely deal for everyone!' with a slightly mad look in his eyes.

'It's not really though, is it?' I said to Nan one time when we were watching.

'What do you mean?'

'It's not really a lovely deal for everyone. He paid the man in the factory £10 each for those old lights and now he's sold them for £150 each. That's just a lovely deal for him, isn't it?'

'But the chap in the factory was delighted to get £10 for them,' said Nan.

'But he didn't know how much they were worth. Hugo should have told him.'

'No, love, he's very fair. It's just his business. He has to make money. He's spent years studying antiques and this is his payment for that.'

I know Nan loves Hugo so I didn't say anything else, but it seems like a bit of a con to me.

Now, when Nan's not watching Hugo on telly she's out at a car boot sale or charity shop looking for some hidden treasure to sell online. Sometimes she's lucky and she'll maybe make £20 or £30 and that makes her really happy, but some stuff doesn't sell at all and it's getting really hard to get my bike out of the shed because of all the rubbish in there. Last week she got very excited about a rotten-looking rocking horse that was missing a leg.

'That'll be worth a fortune to the right buyer,' she said, as she stuffed it in on top of a broken stool. I wondered who the right buyer could possibly be.

I turn to Max now and say, 'I'm not recommending *Treasure Hunters* by the way. You're better off sticking to the Wildlife Channel.'

When the bell rings for home time we head out to the cloakroom. We're just walking past the lockers when Max starts doing a weird kind of dance – patting herself all over like the scary Morris Dancers they had at the Summer Fair last year.

'What are you doing?'

'My phone!'

Turns out she isn't dancing. 'Didn't you get it at home time?' Mr Probert collects everyone's mobile phones in a big plastic box each morning and then returns them to us at the end of the day.

'I don't put it in the box. It could go missing.'

'Where did you put it?'

'The inside pocket of my coat.'

'So … where is it now?'

'I dunno … it's missing!'

'But…' I'm not sure I'm understanding correctly. 'You don't leave valuables in coat pockets. I mean, everyone knows that, don't they? It's basic crime prevention.'

'But it was my *inside* pocket! It has a zip!'

'A zip? What, with a lock on it?'

'No, just a zip.'

'A zip?' I say again.

'Yes! A zip!'

'But … have you ever seen a bank use zips to keep out robbers? Do you zip your door locked at night? Zips are…'

'Lori! Someone's taken my phone!' Max shouts.

I decide to stop talking about zips. Sometimes I think Max is a genius and sometimes, like right now, I'm really not sure.

'Ok.' I feel my heart beating fast. This is what I've trained for. 'We need to act fast. This whole area,' I say, gesturing to the cloakroom, 'is now a crime scene and we need to secure it.' I start running through a mental checklist of all the things I need to do. I get out my secret notebook.

'What are you doing?' says Max.

'Making a list of what we'll need for the scene of crime examination. We need hazard tape, a fingerprint kit…'

'Lori…'

'…camera, evidence bags, tape measure…'

'Lori!'

'What is it?'

'We don't need any of that stuff.'

'But it's a crime scene. There are procedures we need to follow.'

'Come on. We just need to use your nan's laptop. Let's go.'

CHAPTER FOUR

As they walk to Lori's house, Max fumes about the phone. Mostly she fumes at herself. She's only had it a few days and already she's lost it. She imagines what her mum will say. She pictures the disappointment on her face. Her mum's got enough on her plate already now they have to move house. Yesterday she didn't get up for work. She said she couldn't work and look for a flat at the same time so she stayed in bed making phone calls all day. Today she didn't get up again even though she had no more numbers to call. She said she didn't feel well. Max worries about her mum worrying. When her mum worries she gets stressed and when she gets stressed she gets depressed and when she gets really depressed she's not really like Max's mum anymore, she just sits in her dressing gown all day long and can't really speak. And now Max has gone and let someone steal her phone.

Lori's nan makes the girls a cup of tea and gives Max a big pile of coconut ring biscuits on the side. Max loves Lori's nan and particularly loves the way Lori's nan is always trying to fatten her up. Nan goes and fetches her laptop and puts it on the table.

'Here you go, love. You know what you're doing, don't you?' she says.

'I still think it was a mistake not to examine the crime scene more thoroughly,' says Lori.

'We don't need to,' says Max. 'I set up *Find My Phone*.'

'What's that?' say Lori and her nan at the same time.

'It's an app. If your phone goes missing you can look it up online – it shows you the location of your phone on a map.'

'No!' exclaims Lori's nan in astonishment. 'Did you hear that Lori?' She asks even though Lori obviously did hear it as she's sitting right next to Max. 'That's incredible! That could change my life, that could. The amount of time we waste looking for my glasses, or my handbag or my purse. Oh, do you remember that Magic Singing Ringing keyring love?'

'The Magic-Find-That-Key keyring,' Lori corrects.

'Yes, that's what I said. What a palaver that was! Anyway, the thing is, Max, poor Lori is always searching for stuff for me. She says they're not the kind of investigations she wants to be doing! Well, this is the answer, isn't it, Lori love...'

'It only works on smartphones,' says Max, before Nan gets too excited.

'Oh,' says Nan. 'In that case, excuse me while I go and track down my specs. I had them earlier, I know I did.'

Max goes to the Find My Phone website and puts in her phone number. 'If we're lucky they won't have turned the phone off yet, or taken out the SIM.'

'Right,' says Lori, sounding uncertain.

'Yes!' says Max. 'Look, it's there!'

Lori looks at the flashing phone symbol on the map.

'That's Swingo Park!' She pauses. 'I had no idea it was a hotspot for criminals!'

Max looks unconvinced. 'I'm not sure it is. It's usually just little kids and ducks there.'

Lori remembers something. 'You know what? This is all beginning to make sense. Nan's friend Mad Marge left her coat in Swingo Park a while back and when she went back to get it, the coat had gone! Just vanished. Person or persons unknown had taken it. Though Nan said she couldn't believe anyone would want a lilac windcheater and they've never demanded a ransom or anything so it's a bit mysterious.'

'Maybe the park keeper just put it in lost property?' says Max.

'But Max,' says Lori pausing for dramatic effect, 'there is no park keeper! What do you reckon to that?'

Max considers for a moment and says, 'I reckon I need to go and find my phone in Swingo Park.'

'Hang on,' says Lori disappearing from the room. She runs upstairs and returns with two small handsets.

'The Kommunicator 150 walkie-talkies!' says Max. 'I'd forgotten about them. Do they still work?'

'Of course they do! Like Nan says, sometimes the old ways are the best. You take one and I'll keep the other one here with me and keep watch on the screen. If the phone moves I'll radio you. Here's a torch as well. You'll need that. And a magnifying glass. Ideally, I'd give you some night-vision goggles too, but it's going to be at least seven months and three weeks before I've saved up enough for them.'

'Thanks,' says Max. 'I've got to go. I need that phone back.'

It's almost dusk when Max reaches the park. There are no toddlers in the playground, or elderly people feeding the ducks. Something about it reminds Max of the time she helped out with the school play. The show was in the evening and it was really weird being in school after dark – walking along empty corridors and seeing the night sky through the classroom windows. The park is usually so bustling and busy it feels almost spooky now it's deserted. Max sees no one at all as she runs along the side of the pond and up the slope on the far side of the park. When she reaches the bandstand she stops to catch her breath and look around. The loud crackle of the walkie-talkie in her pocket makes her jump as Lori's voice rings out:

'Come in, Ellington. Are you receiving, Ellington?'

'Yes!' She fiddles with the volume. 'Loud and

clear.' Max speaks quietly, nervous of making too much noise.

'Any updates?'

'No. Has the phone moved?'

'No, hasn't budged. You need to look around for suspicious characters. Anyone acting shiftily? Someone carrying a rolled-up umbrella on an otherwise dry day? Wearing sunglasses when the outlook is cloudy?'

Max looks around the deserted park. 'What?'

'Disguises. Anyone around you just look a little bit odd?'

'Lori, there's no one else here. At all.' She whispers, 'It's a bit creepy.'

'Maybe you should come back.' Lori sounds worried. 'Remember Marge's coat – there could be criminals at large there.'

Max starts shining the torch in nearby bushes, looking to see if the phone has been dumped somewhere. The walkie-talkie crackles again.

'What are you doing now?'

'I'm looking for the phone!'

'Good. Are you using the magnifying glass?'

'I'm not sure that would help. The park's quite big.'

'It says on the screen that the location is only approximate. I wonder how approximate.'

Max lifts her head and takes in the expanse of the park. 'I don't know,' she says.

Lori has an idea. 'Why don't…'

Max interrupts. 'If you're going to say "Why don't you come back", I can't, Lori! I've got to find this phone, even if it takes all night.'

'No, I was going to say: why don't I use my phone to call your number? You might be able to hear the ringing.'

Max stops foraging around on her hands and knees and stands up. 'Oh. Yeah. OK. Good thinking, Detective.'

'Hang on, I'll just go and get it.' says Lori and then a moment later. 'OK, here goes.'

Max stands completely still; she can hear the traffic in the distance from New Heath High Street; and she can hear the wind blowing through the leaves of the trees. She shivers slightly and then hears a dog in the distance. It takes a moment to register: it's her ringtone! She set it as a recording of Fang barking. The sound comes from behind her, down the slope near the pond. She starts to follow the sound and then it stops. Suddenly she sees the silhouettes of two figures separate from the dark shadow of the boathouse. She feels goose pimples rise on her arms. The two people run in opposite directions. One shouts something to the other, but Max can't make out what. She presses the button on the Kommunicator 150.

'Which way is the phone moving?'

Lori comes back straight away. 'It's not. The connection has gone dead. There's no symbol.'

Max hesitates for a moment and then starts running after the closest person.

'Hey, wait!' She shouts. She sees the figure turn to look back at her and then carry on running.

Max is tall and skinny and a very fast runner when she wants to be, which is rarely in PE lessons or races at school when there doesn't seem much point, but very much right now chasing someone who may have her phone which she really needs to get back before her mum finds out and gets even more stressed. Soon she's close enough to make out that the figure is a boy, he makes it as far as the car park before slipping on some wet leaves and falling in a heap. Max is on him in a moment.

'Hey you!' She pulls him up off the ground and then steps back in surprise. 'You?'

CHAPTER FIVE

'Who's that?' calls Nan from the kitchen when the doorbell rings.

'Only Max again,' I call back. Max has radioed ahead with information but I'm not sure how much to tell Nan. I never lie to Nan, but I don't like worrying her.

'She's got another friend from school with her, we're just doing some research.' I call down the corridor. This is more or less true and so I think it's OK. I try and ignore the annoying voice in my head asking how something can be 'more or less' true.

'OK, love, don't be too long. Toad in the hole in forty!'

I open the door and it takes me a moment to recognise the skinny, frightened-looking boy with a grazed chin standing next to Max.

'Taylor!' I say. He looks terrified and his trousers are covered with mud. I hurry Max and him into the front room before Nan sees his trousers and wrestles them off him for the washing machine.

I've had a few minutes since Max radioed to try and set up a professional-looking interview room. I've pushed Nan's Wonders of the World jigsaw to the end of the dining table and replaced it with my battery-operated tape recorder, my notebook and pen. The tape recorder is one of the many excellent things Nan has found at car boot sales. She even managed to find some proper old-fashioned but brand new, still-in-the-cellophane tapes to use with it. So far I've only used them to record practice interviews with Nan (she's very good at playing criminals, especially really blood-thirsty ones) but I stop and start the interviews more than is strictly necessary as I just enjoy the sound and feel of the clunky buttons when you press them down.

Max and I sit on one side of the table and Taylor on the other. I press record and speak quietly into the mic:

'Suspect interview of Taylor Barclay by Lori Mason and Max Ellington.'

'What's that?' says Taylor, looking alarmed.

I'm about to explain but Max cuts in. 'Ignore that. What have you done with my phone.'

'I haven't got it anymore,' he says.

'But you admit you took it, so where is it?'

Taylor says nothing.

'Do you know how much trouble I'll be in if I've lost that phone? I'm not some rich kid who gets a new one every week. Where is it?'

Taylor bites his lip. 'I'm sorry.' Now he starts to cry. Max and I look at each other. This is not how suspect interviews go on telly. I've watched hundreds and hundreds of interrogation scenes and this is turning out to be a lot less fun than I'd imagined. I get Taylor a tissue. Normally it's the victim who cries, not the suspect. Max doesn't look like she's about to cry though. I can't imagine anything making Max cry. I can't help feeling a bit sorry for Taylor and I'm worried that this makes me a bad detective. Then I remember that there's always a nice cop and a nasty cop, a standard tactic in interrogations. I can be the nice one.

'Don't cry,' I say. 'It's just … the phone wasn't yours. Max really needs it back. Just tell us what happened. Criminals always feel better after they've confessed.'

'What? I'm not a criminal!' Taylor looks panicked again.

'Just tell us what happened!' says Max impatiently.

It takes a few moments for Taylor to wipe his eyes and blow his nose and then he begins.

'I have to go to Swingo Park on Friday afternoons after school. I can't go home because my mum's at work and she won't let me in the house when she's not there. She says she can't trust me, that I'll break something or make a mess. She says I have to play with my mates.'

'Who are your mates?' I ask.

Taylor's quiet for a while and then says, 'No one now. I had one at my old school – Jake – but I don't see him anymore…' He gives a long sniff. 'I go to the park because there's nowhere else to go. I don't even like it there. It's rubbish if it's raining and I never have any money for chips or anything.' He stops to blow his nose again.

'Carry on,' says Max.

'A few weeks ago, there was this older boy there. I noticed him because it's usually just little kids and their mums. He started coming over to me and I thought it was trouble.'

'What do you mean?' I ask.

He bites his lip. 'I used to get picked on a bit at

my old school. They called me Shrimp. I thought it was going to be that kind of thing.'

'Was it?' I ask.

Taylor shakes his head. 'He came over and asked me what I was doing. I kept thinking he was going to hit me or something, but he was just being friendly. He said his name was Calum.'

I'm puzzled. 'Why wasn't he at school?'

'He goes when he feels like it he said. He thinks school's a waste of time. He thinks we're dead lucky having Friday afternoons off. Anyway, he showed me some stuff on his phone. Some funny videos and things like that. Then he showed me a game he liked. He let me have a go but I was rubbish on it. I never played it before, don't even have a phone. He didn't believe me when I told him that. He said, "You need a phone mate, then we can play even when we're not together."' Taylor pauses a minute and then says, 'He kept calling me mate.'

'So you stole my phone just so you could play some stupid game?' Max interrupts.

Taylor shakes his head. 'No, it wasn't like that. The next time I saw him he said, 'Mate, can you do me a favour?' He told me that he had to go into school for a meeting with the head teacher. I think he was in trouble, I don't know. At his school though he said you're not allowed phones at all. They search you and everything and then they take them off you if they find them. So he asked me if I could look after his phone for an hour or so till he came back. He told me I could practise on the game; he said I needed it.' He pauses. 'He said he wouldn't ask just anyone, but he trusted me.'

'So I said OK. I was only going to be sitting in the park anyway. So he went and it was alright for a bit. I just sat on the bench trying to play that game. Pretending the phone was actually mine. Then this bloke on a bike appeared. Not exactly a bloke but probably too old for school – about 17 or 18 maybe.'

'Who was he?' I ask.

'I don't know. He got off his bike and came straight over to me. He gave my head a push and I knew then I was in trouble. He said 'Phone'. I didn't even understand him at first. Then he said 'Phone. Now.' And held out his hand. I told him it wasn't mine, I was looking after it for someone else. He said he wasn't messing about.' Taylor suddenly starts sobbing. 'He said he had a knife.' Max and I look at each other. 'He grabbed the phone and went.'

We're all silent. I pass Taylor some more tissues. Max waits for him to calm down.

'What happened then?'

He gives a long sniff. 'Calum came back. I told him straight away what happened. I told him we needed to go to the police, but he was like a different person. He wasn't friendly anymore. He just kept shouting at me and giving me little pushes. He said we couldn't go to the police because his dad gave him the phone and he got it off some bloke in the pub and it was probably stolen in the first place. He kept going on about it being a Samsung Galaxy something and it was all my fault it was gone. He didn't even believe the mugger had a knife. He said I was a chicken who didn't even fight back. He said his dad was going to kill him and I owed him the money to buy a new phone. He told me I had to meet him today to pay him back or he'd batter me.'

I write in my notebook: 'Calum = not very understanding.'

Taylor looks from Max to me and back again. 'I didn't know what to do. I don't have any money. I'm skint.' He looks away and says quietly, 'Then I saw you looking at your phone this morning before school. I saw you left it in your pocket. I was desperate. I just thought I'd give that one to Calum to pay him back.'

'So he's got it now?' says Max.

Taylor nods slowly. 'He said it was rubbish though. He was all angry again and pushing me about. Said it was nowhere near as good as the one I lost. But then he calmed down a bit and said maybe it was a start. He said there'd definitely be better phones at school and I needed to bring him some of those – see if they might work out to the same value. He said it was obviously easy to steal them. He started acting like we were mates again – he said I owed him and friends had to pay their debts. I tried to explain I couldn't steal any others, I told him about Probert's box but then your phone starting barking like a dog and he grabbed it from me and ran. He called to me – meet him same time and place next week.' Taylor takes a deep breath and looks at us both again. 'I don't know what to do.'

Max stares at him for a while. 'Do you know where Calum lives?'

Taylor shakes his head.

I look at them both. 'We have to go the police. It sounds like Calum's phone was stolen in the first place and his dad is some kind of criminal. We need to tell someone.'

'No!' says Taylor. 'Please. I've stolen a phone. I'm the one who's in trouble. My mum would kill me.'

Max is looking at Taylor closely. She seems less angry now, more resigned. 'He's right.'

We're silent for a moment and then Max says, 'We need a plan.' She looks at Taylor. 'You, don't say anything to anyone and don't steal any more phones!'

'Calum's going to kill me. Or my mum's going to kill me.'

'Or I'm going to kill you!' says Max, then she sees how frightened Taylor looks. 'Look, no one is killing you yet. Just do nothing till we say so.'

Taylor seems only now to properly take in the notebook and the tape recorder for the first time. He looks at me.

'What is all this stuff?'

I close my notebook in what I think is a very business-like way. 'Paperwork. Totally confidential. This is a professional operation.'

'Lori!' comes the sound of Nan's voice. 'Toad in the hole being served now!'

CHAPTER SIX

Max lies on her bed with Fang on top of her. She updates him on the phone situation.

'...So we need a plan. Any ideas?'

Fang makes a snuffling noise.

'Lori? Yeah, she's bound to come up with something. Maybe she'll remember some old detective story where the same thing happens. Well, not exactly the same – probably not a missing mobile phone, probably a diamond or a priceless antique.'

Fang cocks his head to one side.

'Hmmm? Oh, they're just the kinds of things that used to get stolen before mobile phones were invented.'

Fang puts his head back down in her lap.

'You're right. The main thing is not to worry Mum. I don't want to lie to her ... but it's not lying if I just don't mention the phone, is it? She's got enough on her plate.'

Fang sits right up at the mention of a plate.

'Oh no – dinner! We forgot to eat! Come on, let's go see what's in the kitchen.'

Fang barks and wags his tail following Max down the corridor. She opens the fridge and then each of the cupboards in turn.

'OK, I don't think Mum's had a chance to go shopping. But look – we've got custard creams! Do you want to share them?'

Fang is whining at the fridge door.

'What? It's not a balanced meal? But, they've got custard in them!'

Fang continues to whine.

'Alright, alright, you're right. I know – vitamins, minerals, proper doggy nutrients, you need all that stuff. It's a shame you don't get school dinners like me.' She ruffles his head. 'Let's see if Mum's got some money and we'll go walkies to the shops'.

Angela is up and bustling about in her room packing things in a suitcase while singing quietly to herself. Max notices straight away how carelessly her mum is throwing things in the case and how she keeps singing the same line over and over. She's seen her like this before. Max feels uneasy. She wishes her dad was there.

'What you doing, Mum? I thought you were having a rest.'

'Oh, Maxie, sweetheart.' Her mum beams at her. 'God is smiling on us again!' Max feels a twinge in her stomach. Angela is not normally religious. When she starts talking about God it's sometimes a sign that she's not well.

'I just had a phone call. Everything's going to be fine again baby – thank God! We've got somewhere new to live.'

'But … that's great,' says Max, flooded with relief at the good news. 'When are we going to look at it?'

'Oh, we're not,' says Angela. 'I had to say yes over the phone without seeing it, but I saw some photos on the website and the deposit was affordable, not like most of the others I've seen. It's over on the Glebe estate so not too far from school.' Her mum laughs as if she's nervous and Max frowns at her.

'Is everything OK, Mum?'

'Yes. Didn't you hear me? We've got a new home. Everything's good. You just need to be a big girl and help me.'

'Course I will. Shall I get the boxes down

from on top of the wardrobe?' Max pulls a chair over.

'I don't mean packing,' says her mum.

'What then? What can I do?'

Her mum won't look at her. She carries on piling things in the case: odd shoes on top of underwear, jumpers mixed in with jewellery.

'Your attitude, Max. I need you to be a big girl and have a big-girl attitude.'

Max feels like she's missing something. She's confused. 'OK…' she says.

'You don't want to make things harder for me, do you?'

'No! I never do that.'

'Cos it's been a real struggle finding somewhere new and I've missed work and, to be honest, I've not been feeling good.'

'I know, Mum. Have you spoken to Dad at all? It'll be OK now. We've got somewhere new. We can make it nice.'

Her mum doesn't seem to hear her. 'Because you know, sometimes we have to make sacrifices. Sometimes we have to make changes. Your dad would say the same thing. Everyone has to do it. No special exceptions.'

Max feels a flicker of annoyance. It's as if her mum has forgotten how well Max knows all this already; as if she doesn't know Max at all. 'I know that, Mum. I remember all the places we've lived. I don't complain. If it's one bedroom I don't care. I'll sleep on the sofa. Whatever.'

'It's two bedrooms…'

'Well, that's great then…'

Her mum stops what she's doing and looks at her for the first time. 'It's two bedrooms but…' She starts to cry. Max can't move. She suddenly knows exactly what her mum is about to say. 'But strictly no dogs. Fang can't come.'

Max stands unmoving.

'I tried so hard, Maxie. I swear I tried, but nowhere wants dogs or cats. They're so strict on it. They do spot checks. We needed somewhere to live, sweetheart.'

Max is rigid while her mum hugs her tightly and says the word 'sorry' over and over. Max hears Fang whimpering and feels his warm body rubbing around her ankles.

CHAPTER SEVEN

Mr Meacham stands behind the counter of his sweet shop. It's his quiet time of day, after the morning school rush has died down. Peggoty the cat lies snoring quietly next to the radiator. She has a nice life thinks Mr Meacham, not a worry in the world. Stroked and fussed over by every customer and the rest of the day spent eating or sleeping. Sometimes when the shop's empty Mr Meacham wonders if he needs to update. *Meacham's* doesn't sell cigarettes, or lottery tickets, or groceries or wine or any of the many other things most corner shops sell. 'Sweets' is what's painted on the window and sweets (along with crisps and pop) is all he sells. It seems a bit late to change now. He's been selling sweets for over thirty years. Stick to what you know, he thinks. And he does know sweets. He's not the type to boast, but he's considered something of an expert in confectionery. People travel from far and wide in search of half-remembered sweets of their childhood. Mr

Meacham knows his 'Rosy Apples' from his 'Spanish Gold' sweet tobacco. He's just started on a stock inventory of his loose sweets when the bell over the door jangles and one of his regulars comes in.

'Morning, Max!' calls Mr Meacham. He considers Max one of his very best customers and by that he doesn't mean that she spends the most. In fact, she hardly ever has any money, not like the other kids, but she's a true connoisseur. She has, in Mr Meacham's estimation, a very fine confectionery palate, able to distinguish even between different brands of the same sweet. She's adventurous too, she doesn't just stick to what she knows or what she likes, but eagerly embraces new flavours and combinations. Mr Meacham lets her buy individual sweets rather than whole bags, to allow her meagre budget to stretch further. He also sometimes gives her free sweets to test in exchange for her feedback.

As soon as the door opens today though Mr Meacham sees there is something not right about Max. For one thing, she is not at school. For another, she doesn't have her little dog with her. And for a third she doesn't ask after Peggoty, of whom she's very fond. She doesn't speak at all or even acknowledge Mr Meacham in any way. Instead she stands in front of his wall of jars and stares blankly at the labels. Mr Meacham decides to leave her be but keeps a discreet eye on her. Ten slow minutes later Max hasn't moved or uttered a world. To Mr Meacham's eyes she seems lost in a world of her own. He sits and thinks. He's not a teacher or a counsellor and he never had children of his own. He has no expertise at all in this kind of situation but he can see that something is wrong and he doesn't like it. He resorts to the one thing he does know: confectionery.

Mr Meacham gets off his high stool and places it on the other side of the till. He walks over to the wall of jars and without a word opens several of them and removes a single sweet from each. He lays the sweets out in a line on the counter. He spends a little time arranging them in different sequences until he's sure he has the perfect combination. He approaches Max gently.

'If you'll permit me.' Max jumps at his voice. He smiles to reassure her and gestures towards the stool. 'Please ... take a seat.' Max walks without a word and sits down. He taps on the counter to draw her attention to the line of sweets and then clears his throat:

'One Royale Rhubarb and Custard. One Sherbet Pip. One Satin Pillow. One Sour Apple Cube. One Barley Twist. One Pear Drop, Small.'

Max looks at the sweets and then at Mr Meacham.

'Eat,' he says simply. 'It's a prescription.'

Max starts at the left and slowly works her way along the line, sucking, chomping and chewing, quite miserably at first. Mr Meacham leaves her to it, surreptitiously checking every now and then to see how she's progressing. He notices the blank look in her eyes seems to fade a little with each sweet. When she finishes the final pear drop she remains on the stool but glances up and for the first time that day catches Mr Meacham's eye.

'Hello there,' he says.

She blinks.

'Righto, well, I'll go first then, shall I?' Mr Meacham says. 'Let's start with this: shouldn't you be at school today?'

Max says nothing.

'Are you sick? You don't look too bright.'

She shakes her head.

'Well, if you're not sick, I don't want to worry you, but you are very late. It's almost 10 o'clock.'

'I'm not going to school.' Max finally speaks.

'I see.'

'Ever.'

'Right,' says Mr Meacham.

They sit in slightly awkward silence for what seems ages. Eventually they both speak at the same time. 'Can I ask why?' says Mr Meacham.

'We're losing Fang,' says Max.

Mr Meacham puts down his duster. 'Oh no, Max. That's terrible news. Is he very ill?'

She shakes her head. 'We've got to move and there's no dogs allowed.'

'No dogs allowed? Well, that's ridiculous, isn't it? He's only a little fella. He wouldn't do any damage.'

'I want to run away with him ... but I can't leave Mum behind,' Max says miserably.

'No. I don't think that would be a good idea.'

'Mum says we all have to make sacrifices.'

Mr Meacham looks at Max. 'But some people seem to have to make lot more than others, don't they?'

Max is pale, she looks sickly. Mr Meacham shakes his head. 'I don't think you can lose that dog, can you? I think it might be too hard even for you.' Max says nothing. Silence returns but an idea starts to form in Mr Meacham's head. 'Hang on, you know … there might be a way.'

'There isn't. Mum said. I have to say goodbye.'

'But maybe not goodbye forever.'

'Mum says there's no way the agency will change their mind.' She pauses. 'I hate the agency.'

'Never mind the agency,' says Mr Meacham. 'What about that little friend of yours, the one who's always scribbling things in her notebook.'

Max looks at him. 'Lori? What about her?'

'Yes, Lori, of course. Well, I have the pleasure of knowing Mrs Southwell.'

'Lori's nan?'

'Yes, Pam – she's told me I can call her that – Pam is a delightful lady and I happen to know she is very fond of animals.'

'Yeah, she is.'

'When Peggoty here went missing for a few terrible days it was Mrs Southwell … Pam … who helped track her down.'

'Oh … yeah … she used to help her friend Mad Marge with the missing pet website.'

'Well, look, the thing is I've been rather hoping for another opportunity to speak to Pam, get to know her a little better, and I believe what we have here might be what they call a "coincidence of wants".'

Max blinks at him. 'I have no idea what you're talking about.'

He smiles. 'Would you happen to have Lori's phone number on you?'

She nods. 'It's in my head. I always remember numbers.'

'Course you do. You tell me the number. I'll give Pam a call, and we'll see if we can sort this out.'

CHAPTER EIGHT

I'm peering out of the kitchen window at the garden. 'What exactly do you think he's doing?'

Nan glances out. 'He's exploring. Leave him to it.'

I carry on watching. Fang has been living with us for three days now. I've spent a lot of that time watching him like this. 'Is it normal for dogs to explore so much or is he … special?'

'Oh, it's normal.' She says, carrying on with the washing up.

'Right.' I watch as the dog now starts digging up the lawn. I wonder what he's hoping to find. I mean explorers usually discover new continents, or planets or lost treasure. Fang just seems to discover rubbish. Or at least it's become rubbish by the time he's finished with it. Like our post for example, which is now just our daily pile of shredded paper.

'There are all kinds of new smells for him here, love,' says Nan, 'and that's how dogs learn about their surroundings. Smell is very important to them. He's just finding his way in a new home.'

'I see.' I say, but I'm not sure that I do.

'You don't have to worry about him at all, he's still Max's responsibility, she still takes him on his walks and feeds him … he just … lodges with us. I don't know why you can't just ignore him.'

Ignore him is the last thing I can do. I have started a list in my notebook:

Pros and cons of fostering a dog

Pros:

1. *Max doesn't lose dog.*
2. *Max comes to visit twice a day every day.*
3. *Dog keeps Nan company when I'm at school.*

Cons:

1. *I have to listen to Max's 'conversations' with dog. Both Max and Nan have a strange belief that the dog understands English.*
2. *Dog keeps 'exploring' in my room, has chewed some of my case files and slobbered on my books.*

3. *Dog has sharp teeth.*
4. *Dogs can smell fear.*

It's not that I'm scared of dogs. Obviously. I mean, who's ever heard of a private detective who's frightened of household pets? That would be ridiculous. So, no, not scared. Not always anyway. Dogs just make me a bit nervous. Particularly the way they jump up on you and bark loudly and 'nip playfully'. Nan says Fang's just being friendly when he does those things and seems to forget that I've grown up in a world where jumping up at someone and giving them a little bite on the nose isn't a sign of friendliness, it's more often a sign that you need to call the police. I understand that shaking hands isn't an option for a dog, but surely there's a middle way? Maybe a gentle paw press on the shin? A friendly nod of the head? Anything that doesn't involve barking, tongues or teeth would be a big improvement. Naturally I've started compiling a dossier on Fang. I'm keeping a very close eye on his behaviour. It's not that I consider him criminal, but he is a person (or dog more accurately) of suspicion. I pull out my notebook now and make a quick entry:

8.45am
Dog destroying lawn.

My pencil hovers over the page but I can think of nothing more to add. I can offer no insight or motivation. I'm distracted from dog surveillance by the doorbell.

'That'll be Max,' says Nan and I go and let her in.

'How's my boy this morning?' says Max, as soon as the door opens.

'Oh, hi Max,' I say, but she's already walked straight past me to look for the dog.

By the time I get to the garden Max and Fang are in the middle of one of their twice daily, quite emotional reunions. I see the pile of earth Fang has dug up in the middle of the lawn and go over to inspect. There is a large hole in the centre of the garden. I kneel down to try and see how deep it goes. Max walks over.

'He explores by his sense of smell.'

'Yes, so I've heard.'

'Probably found a bone. He's a hunter.'

'A bone?' I find this idea quite alarming. 'Why would we have bones buried in our garden?'

Fang races over and starts barking crazily at the hole, trying to jump in and dig more. Max holds him back.

'Well, there's something down there that he's interested in.'

'Hmmm.' I pick up a stick and give a few little pokes down the hole. I can actually feel something flat and hard. 'There is something.'

'Does it feel like a bone?' says Max, as if I have lots of experience of identifying bones with sticks.

'I don't think so. It feels flat, more like a box.'

She pats him on the head. 'Well done, Fang.' She seems to be praising him for what is basically an act of vandalism. 'Come on, it's time for your walk,' she says attaching the lead.

'Don't forget our interview with Taylor tomorrow,' I say. 'We need to get a good description of this Calum character.'

'I know,' she says, but her mind is more on the dog as she rubs the side of his face. 'Come on, boy, let's go and see what we can find.'

After they've gone, I go back in the kitchen and eat a bowl of Rice Krispies. I try to forget about Fang and the hole but it's no good. I keep thinking about the feel of the flat object under the lawn. In the end I put my spoon down.

'Great, now I'm turning into a dog,' I say to no one in particular and go out to the shed to find a trowel. I kneel down by the hole and start excavating carefully. After a few moments I've uncovered the top of something, but I don't know what.

I dig around the sides and then manage to prise up from the soil what turns out to be a small oblong Tupperware box. I'm a bit disappointed. I don't know what I was expecting, maybe not an actual treasure chest, but something a little more exciting than a school lunch box. I pick it up and can tell by the weight that there's something inside. Could it be a historically significant sandwich from decades ago? Then a terrible thought occurs to me. Maybe Max was right about the bones. Maybe the garden is a cemetery – a pet cemetery! Maybe inside lies a beloved, dead pet. I put the box down quickly. This situation calls for Nan.

Nan is physically incapable of seeing a speck of dirt without needing to clean it immediately. Fang is having to get used to this. When she sees a soil encrusted lunch box plonked in the middle of the dining table she's all over it in seconds with J cloths and anti-bacterial sprays. This though actually turns out to be a very good course of action, as once cleaned, we see that the lunchbox is red and Nan goes, 'Aha!'

'Aha, what?' I say.

'There's no dead pet in there.'

'How do you know?' I say.

'Because I recognise it, now all that filth's off it, don't you? Look!' She goes over to the big kitchen drawer and pulls out another matching box in a slightly larger size. 'It's one of your mum and dad's love. Good quality stuff. We still use the other one. Now, they definitely never had any pets, so there's no danger of finding a mummified guinea pig in there. Go on, open it up, love, whatever it is. Let's see it.'

Nan stands poised with the anti-bac spray like a cowboy with a gun as I open the box. The first thing I see is a label stuck to the inside of the lid. I read the words out loud. '*Time Capsule. Buried: October 4 2009 to mark the one-month anniversary of Loretta Mason's birth. To be opened at her 18th birthday party.*'

Nan sits down heavily on a chair. I stare at the words.

'Is this ... is this from my mum and dad?'

Nan can't speak for a moment. She nods and then says, 'That's just the sort of daft thing they'd do. Oh, they loved you so much, sweetheart.'

I don't remember my mum and dad at all. They died when I was four months old. That's when Nan came to look after me. It's weird to think of them burying this box for me to find one day. Weird to think they imagined they'd be with me when I found it. I start to reach in and then stop and look at Nan.

'I'm not 18. Do you think I should wait?'

Nan looks at me. 'Things didn't turn out the way your mum and dad planned. I think you've waited long enough already. Go ahead.'

I start taking things out and putting them on the table. There is a tiny pair of striped knitted booties; a pencil drawing of a baby asleep; a lock of hair tied with a thin, turquoise ribbon; a splodgy hand print in gold paint on a piece of black card and a hospital wristband which says: '*765 387 5589. Baby Mason. Female. 3020g*'.

Nan holds the drawing gently in her hand.

63

'That would have been your dad who did that. He was very artistic.' Nan's crying a bit. She looks from the picture to me. 'I remember you just like that, love.' She squeezes my hand. I notice one last thing in the box. I reach in and hold it up.

'Nan, look!'

She frowns before recognising what it is. 'Oh, it's a dongle thingy!'

'A memory stick!' I say, as I run to get the laptop.

I rush back and fumble a little with the USB stick trying to put it in. The folder contains just one video file. I click and the screen fills with an image of our lounge. I can tell from the angle of the sunlight that it's morning. Everything looks just the same – the same pictures hanging on the walls, the same books on the shelves, the same big red rug on the floor and the same comfy grey chairs on either side of the fireplace. Everything looks the same but completely unfamiliar because sitting in the grey chairs are two people I've never seen sitting there before; two strangers: my mum and my dad.

My mum holds a baby on her lap. I've seen videos of my parents before, odd bits from holidays or special occasions on Nan's phone or laptop but this is different. Here they are, in our house, on our chairs, talking directly to me. Except now I notice that they're not. I've been so wrapped up in what I see that it's only now I realise there's no sound. My parents' lips move but no words come out.

'What are they saying?' I blurt out, as if Nan could possibly tell me.

'Must have got damaged being in the ground all those years,' says Nan.

I watch my mum and dad's faces move. I put my face to the screen. 'I can't hear you.' I whisper to my parents.

CHAPTER NINE

Taylor's coat is too big for him. The sleeves hang down below his hands. It makes him look even skinnier and smaller than he is. He is extra slow putting it on after school on Friday. All of the other children have already left for the day. He looks at the clock in the corridor: 1.05pm. It's another four hours before he's allowed to go home. Mr Probert leaves the classroom and sees Taylor lingering in the cloakroom.

'Everything OK, Taylor?'

'Yes sir,' says Taylor.

'Are you sure?' says Mr Probert. 'You've seemed a bit distracted the last few days. I've been wanting to talk to you. I know it's not easy settling in to a new school. You know that you can tell me if there's a problem.'

Taylor nods his head and zips up his coat quickly. 'I know, sir. There isn't a problem.' He walks quickly away.

'Take care. Have a good weekend,' Mr Probert calls after him.

As Taylor turns out of the school gates he feels someone walking behind him. He freezes, turns around slowly and then breathes out.

'I thought you were him.'

Max shakes her head. 'Just reminding you to stay away from Swingo Park.'

'I don't need reminding. I haven't thought about anything else all week.'

'Where are you going to go?'

'Poundland,' says Taylor.

'You can't spend four hours in Poundland!' says Max.

'I can try.'

'Have you got any money?'

'No.'

'Well, the security guard will start following you round after about fifteen minutes and then he'll kick you out.'

'Oh.'

'Why don't you go to the library?'

Taylor looks as if this is a mad suggestion. 'The library? I don't even have a card.'

'You don't need one. Anyone can go. There's no security guards and you don't need money. You can look at books or comics and they've got heating.'

Taylor looks dubious. 'I don't know.'

'Trust me. The library's alright. And you're not going to see Calum in there.'

Taylor shudders visibly at the mention of Calum's name. 'Alright. Maybe I'll try it.' He hesitates. 'I'm sorry, you know … about your phone.'

'I know,' says Max.

'Thanks for not telling.'

She shrugs. 'Grown-ups don't always help.' She pauses. 'What would your mum do if she found out?'

Taylor sighs. 'I dunno. Depends on the day. Somedays she just shouts. Says I'm no good. Other days she loves me.'

'Maybe she's just stressed.'

'Yeah. I know, it's my fault. I stress her, she says. I give her a headache, just the sight of me. I just try and keep in my room so she doesn't get mad.'

Max looks at him. 'It's not. You know that, don't you?'

He frowns. 'What's not?'

'It's not your fault.' She's about to say something else but then sees Lori up ahead waiting for them at the corner.

'Did you get a good description?' She asks Max when they reach her.

'Oh – not yet. I was just going to ask him.'

'Ask what?' says Taylor.

Lori gets out her notebook and pen and clears her throat. 'We need an accurate description of Calum.'

Taylor looks nervous. 'What for?'

'Surveillance.'

'Well … I don't know … he's just kind of normal looking.'

Lori waits and when she realises nothing more is coming, says, 'Shall I try asking you questions?'

Taylor nods. 'OK.'

'Right … how tall is he?'

'Erm … average.'

Lori looks at him. 'Is he taller or shorter than you?'

'Taller.'

'By how much?'

Taylor looks anxious. 'Sorry. I don't know. I'm not very good at measurements.'

'Right.' She writes this down in her notebook. 'Hair?'

'Yes.' Taylor nods positively.

'What?' says Lori.

'He definitely has hair,' Taylor says with some confidence. '100 per cent definite'.

Max tries not to smile.

'Can you tell me what colour his hair is, please?' says Lori.

'Oh, right … brown. I think. Actually, not sure. He wears a cap.'

'Any emblem or embellishment on the cap?'

'What?'

Max translates. 'What's the brand?'

'Oh … it's Nike.'

Lori makes a note of that. 'Any spectacles, hearing aids, walking sticks or other physical aids?'

'What? No! I don't think so.'

'Does he limp?'

'No.'

'Clothing?'

'Yes. Definitely.'

Lori looks at him and then speaks slowly. 'Can you describe the clothes, please?'

'Oh right, yeah. Erm … usual.'

'Usual?'

'Yeah, you know, the usual things kids wear.'

Lori stares at him until he finally adds, 'So, black school trousers, black hoodie.'

'Thank you,' says Lori. She reads back over her notes. 'So, he's normal height. He has hair, but colour unknown. Wears a cap and a hoodie.'

'That's basically every boy in New Heath,' says Max.

Taylor thinks and eventually says, 'He carries a JD duffle bag on his back.'

Max nods. 'OK, that narrows it down to 95 per cent of the boys in New Heath.'

Lori closes her pad.

'Sorry,' says Taylor. 'I'm not very good at describing.'

'Observing really,' says Lori. 'Poor observation skills. Don't feel bad. I've had years of training. Thanks for your assistance anyway.'

Taylor looks at them both. 'What are you going to do?'

Max shrugs. 'Get my phone back, of course.'

She heads off with Lori, leaving Taylor to kill the afternoon on his own.

When they are almost at Swingo Park, Lori reaches into her backpack and pulls out a woolly hat and cagoule and puts them both on.

'It's not going to rain, is it?' says Max.

'No. It's a disguise.'

Max considers this. 'But … Calum doesn't know who you are. You don't need a disguise.'

Lori shakes her head. 'It's standard undercover operation procedure. Just blending in.'

Max looks at the blue sky and then at Lori in the hat and cagoule. 'Right,' she says.

They make their way across the park and sit on a bench overlooking the children's play area.

'Remember: just act natural,' says Lori, getting a newspaper out of her bag to read. She sits in her winter wear reading the *Financial Times*. Max opens her mouth to say something, but changes her mind.

Despite Taylor's limited powers of description, it's easy to spot Calum. There's only one person remotely fitting the description in the playground; everyone else is either a toddler or a parent. He sits on the back of a bench looking around.

'That's anti-social behaviour right there, already,' says Lori, peering over the top of her paper.

'What?' says Max.

'Feet on seat – not considering other bench users.'

'Come on. Let's go and talk to him.' Max starts to get up.

'Wait!' says Lori. 'You can't just rush these things! What are we going to say?'

'How about: "Give me my phone back!"'

'I don't know if that's a good idea. Taylor said he gets really angry, he might shout at us, and remember his dad associates with criminals.'

Max suddenly jumps up. 'Look! He's going! Come on, Lori. I don't want to lose him. Let's go.'

Calum jogs over to the car park with Max and Lori running some distance behind. He heads straight for a black car and starts talking to the driver. Calum looks nervous and the man at the wheel seems cross with him. Max stops and watches from a distance. The car is small with tinted windows. Max can see the driver but can't tell if anyone else is inside. Lori catches up with her. Max squints at the car.

'Who's he talking to? I can't talk to him if he's with someone else.'

Lori fiddles with her backpack.

'Lori! Look. He's getting in the back. Oh … we

should do something quick. What do we need to do?'

'Get the registration number...' murmurs Lori.

'Yes! Yes, registration number. I haven't got a pen. If I had my phone I could take a photo but...' She's interrupted by the sound of whirring and clicking. She turns to see Lori holding an old-fashioned-looking camera with a very long lens.

'Hang on,' says Lori, 'just getting some close ups of the driver.'

Max stares in amazement. 'Where did you get that?'

'Nan got it at a car boot sale. It's pretty good for ops like this.'

Max looks at Lori in her bobble hat. Sometimes she can't work out if Lori is brilliant or crazy.

'Good detective work is just a question of being prepared really,' says Lori, putting the camera back in her bag.

Probably brilliant, thinks Max. Today at least.

CHAPTER TEN

I've tried lip reading – squinting at the screen trying to match words to mouth shapes but it's basically impossible. I don't know how anyone does it. Maybe they don't. Maybe lip readers just make it all up. I make a note in my pad to investigate this at some future point. As far as the video goes, though, I've had to give up and try to accept that I'll never know what my parents wanted to say to me. But it's hard.

I still watch the video. I like noticing things about Mum and Dad. For example, my dad is a bit of a fidget. His left leg jiggles up and down when he talks and sometimes he nods his head when my mum is speaking, as if he's listening to music. He finds it hard to keep still. He has a splodge of yellow paint on his left hand. I recognise the colour from my bedroom walls. He is also wearing odd socks. I'm not sure if that is deliberate or not. Nan did say he was artistic.

My mum wears glasses and a stripey T-shirt.

She tugs her earlobe the same way Nan says I do when I'm tired. She smiles a lot. She keeps glancing down though, as if she'd rather look at the baby on her lap than anything else. I know the baby is me, but I still wish she'd look at the camera, look at me now, more. She keeps squeezing the baby's hand and I look at my hand and try and imagine my mum squeezing that. I don't know why, but I don't really like the baby.

I concentrate instead on the familiar things in the room, the pictures on the wall, the books on the shelves. I look at the spines of the vintage crime novels, all of which I've read. All except one. It has a distinctive yellow spine that I don't recognise. I pause the video and go up close to the screen to read:

The Owls of Grey Gardens by Edna Slaney

It's weird. I'm pretty sure I've read all of Edna Slaney's books. I've definitely read all the ones that mum and dad had, but now it looks like they used to have another one. I pause the video and look at the room around me. My mum and dad loved books. They cover two whole walls of the lounge, from floor to ceiling and they are in strict alphabetical order by author. Once when I was younger I made a discovery that even Nan didn't know about. The very last page of every single book in this room is stamped with mum and dad's initials. It's not an inked stamp – you can't really see it unless you tilt the page in the light – but there it is, pressed into the paper: 'J&SM', which stands for Jim and Sylvie Mason. 'Embossed' is what Nan says it's called. I don't know why they did it, but I like it. I work my way through the 'S' section of the books carefully. The Edna Slaney novels are all from the same publisher but each one has a different-coloured spine. There is no yellow one there. I go through all the other shelves. There are plenty of books with yellow spines, but not *The Owls of Grey Gardens*.

In the kitchen Nan is wrapping our sandwiches up in tin foil. I'm about to ask her about the missing book but then she turns around and I'm momentarily startled. 'Gosh! Is that a new hat?'

Nan beams at me. 'Well spotted, Detective Mason! Yes, it's smashing, isn't it?'

'It's … unusual.' The hat is an old-fashioned kind of flat cap. On telly it would be worn by someone from the olden days who worked down a mine or something like that. It's the material though that makes it really stand out. Instead of being made of tweed or wool or whatever, it's made from bright pink and black zebra-striped fun fur.

'I know! I was proud as punch when I found it. Can you tell who I'm modelling myself on?'

I stare at the hat. 'I have honestly no idea.'

'Hugo Smythe, of course! Treasure Hunter extraordinaire! I thought it'd be just the ticket for our trip to the car boot today. He always wears a flat cap on his little outings, but as you know I favour a hat with a little more pizzazz, so when I saw this one, I thought...'

'Pizzazz?'

'Exactly. Come on, are you almost ready? The early bird catches the worm you know.' Nan always says this and one day I should explain to her that it doesn't really encourage me to get to places early. I'm not a big fan of worms. But now is not the time for that.

'Nan, I wanted to ask you: on the video of Mum and Dad there's a book on the shelf but it's not there now. Can you remember any other books in the house?'

'No love, you know that, I've told you before, when I moved in I didn't really change a thing. I left everything just where it was. The only room I changed was the spare room when I moved my stuff in – but to be honest that was just filled with their work stuff and I put it all up in the loft.'

'Yeah, that's what I thought. That's why it's weird.'

'Well, maybe your dad just moved it to make room for other books. He was always buying new books – and when I say new I mean old, of course. "Antiquarian" he called them. He used to go to auctions to bid on them. You should have seen him whenever he won a book he was set on getting. I remember once he told me he'd spent £45 on a single book! And I wouldn't mind but it smelt like it had been kept in a damp cellar for the last fifty years.'

A terrible thought occurs to me. 'The dog wouldn't eat a book, would he?'

'No! Course not. Fang wouldn't do that. I mean … he'd give one a good chew. Possibly eat a page or two, but he'd never manage a whole book.'

I'd be more convinced by this if Fang wasn't barking crazily and bouncing up and down wildly as Nan speaks. He does this every time she fetches her coat in anticipation of an outing.

'Come on then!' she says to both of us. 'We need to get the bus down to Dark Lane.'

I've got used to car boot sales since Nan's gone mad for buying junk. Early most weekend mornings, we're off and out on our way to some field or other on the edge of the city. If you've never been to one, car boots are quite weird to begin with. The first thing you see is bunting and flags and bouncy castles and candy floss vans and it all looks like a funfair. Then you pay your £1 and go through the gate and instead of carousels and waltzers there are just rows and rows of parked cars and slightly miserable and/or tired looking grown-ups shivering in the mud waiting for someone to pay them 50p for some bath salts, or heated curlers. Sometimes there's a butcher with a microphone shouting about all the meat he has on his van too. That's quite strange.

Although they are almost always muddy, often cold and windy, and I'm not really interested in anything for sale, I quite like going booting (as Nan calls it). They are very good places to observe suspicious-looking characters and activity. I always fill at least two pages in my notebook. Today one of the first tables we pass is filled with hundreds and hundreds of used mobile phones. I wonder if they could be stolen. I have a good look through in case I can see Max's phone anywhere. There are a few of the same type but they have different cases. Right next to the phone stall is a massive pile of cuddly toys in a giant heap on a blanket on the ground. The stall holder really hasn't made any effort with merchandising – no sign, no prices, no table and the blanket isn't even waterproof. A big polar bear has rolled off the summit and now lies face down in a muddy puddle, its white fur turning black. Next to the pile is a very surly-looking bald man with a tattoo covering his neck. He doesn't look to me like someone who has ever owned a single cuddly toy, let alone over two hundred of them. Where has he got them from? Is it possible that he's a specialist toy burglar, breaking into houses all over the city in the dead of night and stealing soft toys from the arms of small children? Is there a big criminal network of teddy traffickers? I shudder at the thought.

A lorry at the end of the row is surrounded by a crowd of people rummaging through the tables tops around it. 'What's going on there?' I say to Nan. 'What are they selling?'

'All sorts. It's a house clearance.'

We get closer and I see that Nan's right. The tables are covered with the entire contents of somebody's home – from photo albums and clothes and books, to old knives and forks and even unopened jars of foods. Eager hands grab at everything.

'Aren't you going to look?' I ask as Nan carries on walking.

'No. I can't quite stomach it, love. I'm sure you can find treasure that way, but all I can think of is the poor person who's died. Those are someone's cherished belongings and I don't have their permission to look or buy...' Nan trails off as she notices a man walk away from the house clearance tables. 'Hang on. I recognise him!' The man is extremely tall with brown, curly hair and a dark patch on his face.

'Well, he is quite recognisable.' I say.

'I remember now! He was a friend of your dad's! Come on! I've not seen him in years!'

We catch up with the man and Nan calls out to him.

'Cooeee!' (You might think that old ladies don't actually say 'Cooeee' in real life, but my nan does and often!) 'You there. I'm ever so sorry, love, I've forgotten your name. Yes you! With the hair!'

The man spins round quite suddenly and looks blankly at Nan. 'Can I help you?'

Fang is straining at the lead, trying to jump up and give the man one of his friendly nips, but Nan manages to hold him back.

'Oh, sorry, you've probably forgotten me. One old lady looks just like another. I'm Jim's mother-in-law.'

The man looks at Nan a little impatiently. 'Jim who? I'm sorry, I can't place you.'

'Jim Mason. Jim – your best mate at school. Jim…' Nan seems lost for words. She lowers her voice as if I won't hear, '…who died. Remember? You came to visit us after … Lori here was just a little baby then. She's Jim's daughter.'

'Oh!' says the man slightly uncertainly. 'Jim Mason. My best mate at school. Jim who died. Of course, I'm sorry. My memory's terrible.'

'It's OK, love. I've forgotten your name, too. What was it?' says Nan. This is turning into quite a weird conversation.

'Gordon. Gordon Trent.'

Nan laughs. 'You see! Doesn't even ring a bell now. Terrible memory for names but a brilliant memory for faces. That's me.'

Gordon laughs too. 'Well, you don't forget a face like mine,' he says cheerfully, pointing to the mark on his cheek. From a distance it looked a bit like a tattoo, but up close you can see that it's a birthmark. It's vaguely the same shape as a dog's head or the outline of Australia.

'You been on your travels again, have you?' says Nan.

'Travels?' says the man, as if he's not sure what the word means.

'Where was it? Sri Lanka? Indonesia? Somewhere like that you'd just come back from when we saw you last.'

'Oh, yeah, of course. To be honest, I travel so much, I get the years and places mixed up.' He smiles but doesn't seem to know what to say next. 'Look, I'd love to chat but I was just leaving, I've got to be somewhere. It was lovely to see you

84

again Mrs ... Mason and meet you...' He looks at me but clearly can't remember my name. 'All the best now.'

And he's gone. That seemed a bit awkward even by Nan's standards. Nan talks to random people wherever we go. People at bus stops and in shops, old friends and complete strangers, basically if they've got ears, Nan talks to them. Sometimes it can be a bit embarrassing, especially when the person being chatted to doesn't seem to share Nan's love of small talk, but it makes Nan happy so I say nothing.

'Come on, love,' says Nan. 'I spy a bamboo whatnot at four o'clock. Let's see if I can get it cheap and flog it high to some metropolitan type.'

I have literally no idea what she's talking about. I smile and follow her.

CHAPTER ELEVEN

Max's new flat is on the eighth floor of Measham Tower and she loves the views from her bedroom, especially at night when the street lights come on and she can imagine she's looking out over any city in the world. She thinks the new neighbours seem OK. On one side there's a woman with toddler twins who Max likes to make laugh by playing peepo. On the other side is a couple with lots of tattoos and piercings who always say hello. It's hard living without Fang though. Max misses him most at night. Sometimes she forgets and stretches her toes to feel his warm body, but there's nothing there.

Not all the new neighbours are great. The person in the flat below spends a lot of time screaming at their children and someone on the floor above plays crazily loud music, sometimes all night. Max is getting skinnier running up and down eight flights of stairs every day. She tries to avoid the lift. Sometimes the floor is wet and there are angry handwritten signs that say 'This is a lift, not a toilet!!' Max knows that her mum doesn't like Measham Tower at all. She's having problems sleeping at night, she says the noise makes her nerves bad. She gets stressed about dirt and germs, about people dumping rubbish on the stairways and sometimes she shouts if Max forgets to be careful about not touching the handrails or door handles on the landings.

It's 6.45am and her mum is putting her coat on for work. Max looks out of the living room window:

'You know, people would pay loads of money for views like these, Mum. We're lucky, we basically live in a penthouse apartment.'

Her mum smiles. 'I know. We're luckier than lots of people.'

Max can hear the tiredness in her mum's voice. 'Why don't you try sleeping in my room? It might be quieter than yours.'

'Don't you be worrying about me. I'm fine. You're the one who needs a good night's rest – keep that big brain of yours going.' She pats her pockets to make sure she has everything. 'Now listen, I might be late again tonight. Will you be OK?'

'Yeah, of course I will.'

'Make sure you have your phone on so I can call you if I have to do a double shift.'

'Right,' says Max, trying to avoid her mum's eyes.

'I called you yesterday and it said you couldn't be reached. You've got to make sure you have it charged up!'

Max says nothing and her mum carries on. 'No point you having it, if I can't speak to you. Look, I've got five minutes before the bus. You know what would cheer me up for the day?'

'What?' says Max, eager to know.

'Show me some videos of our boy, Fangie. I miss that little guy so much. What's he up to these days? I bet Lori's Nan's been fattening him up.'

Max feels sick. She knows she can't put the moment of truth off any longer. Her brain is quick enough to think up lots of lies. But her mouth won't let her do it. She swallows and tries to think how best to break the news.

'Wait!' shouts her mum suddenly. 'Oh no, I forgot. I don't have five minutes! I'm late. I've gotta dash.' She runs over and kisses Max. 'Later, honey, OK?'

Crossing the estate on her way to school, Max sees Taylor.

'Hey,' she calls out and notices how he flinches in fright. She catches up with him. 'It's only me.'

'Yeah,' he says and walks on with his head down.

'Hang on. We may as well walk in together. What's up?'

'Calum found me,' he says.

'What? How?' says Max

'He waited for me last night after school. Wanted to know where I'd been on Friday. He said he thought we were mates and why hadn't I met him when I said I would.'

'What did you say?'

'I lied. Said I'd been sick. He said that mates pay their debts, that I still owed him and that the phone I'd given him was rubbish…'

'Mates don't force other mates to steal phones. Somebody needs to tell him that.'

'He said I'd have to do better. What if he's there again tonight, waiting for me?'

'But you've told him you'll turn up this Friday.'

Taylor carries on as if he hasn't heard. 'I begged my mum for the day off school. I told her

I was really sick but she wouldn't have it. She didn't believe me. Even if I was sick she couldn't stand the thought of me being in the house when she's at work.'

'You can't miss school because of this,' says Max.

'And Mr Probert keeps asking me questions. He says he's worried about me; he thinks something's wrong. He keeps telling me that I can talk to him. But I can't.'

'Look,' says Max. 'Lori and me will walk out with you after school this afternoon. If Calum's there he'll leave you alone if you're with other people.'

Taylor looks at her for the first time. 'Will you?'

Max is about to answer when she sees Lori up ahead coming towards them, waving some kind of envelope. She runs up, out of breath.

'Look, I've got the photos.'

Max frowns. 'You said it'd take a week.'

Taylor looks confused. 'What photos? How could they take a week? Asda prints them straight away.'

Max explains. 'No, these are photos from an

old camera – it uses film and you have to post it somewhere to get them developed.'

Taylor pulls a face. 'Well that sounds rubbish.'

Lori ignores this. 'I was wrong. Nan told me – she said that old cameras are making a comeback – you know like vinyl. There's a place in town called Snaps Express – they develop film in an hour!' She pulls the pile of photos out of a paper wallet. 'Look!'

Taylor starts to head off. He turns to Max before he goes. 'So … after school, you'll come out with me, yeah?'

'Hang on,' says Max. 'These are from the park on Friday. You need to look at them and confirm it's Calum.'

Lori flicks through the photos. 'Sorry, my nan was using the camera before I borrowed it. She's been photographing herself in different hats.'

'Wait!' says Max. 'Look! She's taken some of my boy Fang. Oh, look at his face! Look at the intelligence in his eyes. I need a copy of that.'

Taylor shuffles a little impatiently and Max remembers what they're supposed to be doing.

'Right. Yeah, OK – look here we go – here are the ones of the park. You see there, that kid walking towards the car. Is that Calum?' She holds the photo out to Taylor.

'Yeah, that's him.' He nods anxiously, handing the photo back quickly but then stops. 'Hang on.' He looks again and screws his face up. 'What? That doesn't make any sense.'

'What doesn't?' says Max.

'The guy in the car. The one driving.'

'What about him?'

'That's who mugged me. He's the one who nicked Calum's phone!'

The three of them crowd around the photo. Max and Lori both realise at the same time.

'It was a set-up,' says Max.

'What?' says Taylor.

'A staged robbery,' says Lori.

'Fake,' says Max. 'It was a trap. Calum lending you the phone was a trap. That was the bait. Then his mate comes and "mugs" you and then you owe him.'

'But why would he do that? What have I ever done to him?'

Max remembers the way Calum seemed nervous. 'Maybe he didn't have a choice either. Maybe he's trapped too.'

'We really need to go to the police,' says Lori.

Max shakes her head. 'But we haven't got any proof of anything. All the photos show is that Calum knows that bloke in the car. We haven't any proof about who mugged Taylor.'

'How are you going to get that?' says Taylor.

Max thinks for a moment. 'We set a bigger trap.'

CHAPTER TWELVE

I'm trying my best to ignore the dog. I sit in the comfy grey armchair in the lounge re-reading an old Edna Slaney novel while the dog sniffs noisily about the shelves. I'm not succeeding. I read a line, then look up, read a line, then look up. It's pretty much impossible to concentrate on even the most thrilling plot whilst at the same time making sure a dog doesn't start eating books or trying to dig holes in rugs.

Nan's always telling me not to mither about the dog and I'm always telling her that I don't even know what mither means so I'm pretty sure I can't be guilty of it. She says it means to fuss or worry unnecessarily. She says Fang's a good dog and I don't need to watch him all the time. Nan doesn't really understand that the reason I watch Fang all the time isn't because I really care about our rugs, but because I'm frightened to take my eyes off him for too long. The reason she doesn't understand this is because, of course, I've never told her. I'm not only slightly scared of dogs. I'm also slightly embarrassed to admit it. I know Fang isn't the worst kind of dog but at the end of the day he is still a panting, snuffling, tongue-lolling, four-legged creature living with us and to be honest the name doesn't help. *Fang*. Why would anyone call a dog Fang? It's just worrying. I peep over my book and look at his sharp white teeth. I imagine them sinking into my arm. When I tear my eyes away from his teeth, I notice that he's looking right at me, head on one side, as if he can read my thoughts. I speak in a low voice.

'Look, sorry, no offence. It's not that I think you'd actually bite me. It's just your teeth are very sharp and you are an animal and animals can be quite … well, unpredictable … and don't think that just because I'm talking to you I think you understand. I don't. I'm just … thinking out loud.'

'Who are you talking to?' says Nan as she walks in.

'No one. I mean … myself. I mean – I was just thinking out loud.'

'You want to be careful of that,' says Nan. 'That's how Mad Marge started and look at her now. She says that talking to herself is the only way she can have an intelligent conversation – which now I come to think of it is a bit rude.'

'I'm sure she doesn't mean you, Nan.'

'No, you're right. She can't do, can she? Anyway, talking of intelligence, I've just had a bit of a lightbulb moment.'

'What is it?' I say.

'Well, I was thinking about that fella we saw at the car boot the other day and I think I might have solved the mystery of the missing book.'

'Really?'

'Yes, I think you can close the file on it now. Stamp "Case closed" on it or whatever it is that you do.'

'I hadn't actually started a file, Nan. If I started one every time something went missing in this house I'd need a new filing cabinet in a week.'

'I suppose you're right,' she says. 'So anyway, that fella, I've forgotten his name again…'

'Gordon Trent.'

'I knew you'd know! I was thinking about the time I met him before. I remember it now. He actually called at the house. I'd not been living here that long. I'd say it was maybe only a few months after your mum and dad passed away.

Anyway, he came around and said he wanted to pay his respects or however he put it. He'd been living abroad – travelling around Asia or something like that and he'd not long come back when he heard the news.'

'How did he know Mum and Dad?'

'He was at school with your dad. Best friends they were back then apparently and they'd kept in touch over the years. Anyway, it was nice of him to come round. But I remember now that he was very embarrassed. He said he didn't like to ask…'

'Ask what?'

'Well, he said that before he'd gone away, he'd lent your dad a book and he wondered if it would be OK to get it back. He said he wouldn't trouble me normally but it had been a present from his dad, who'd passed away some years ago and it had a bit of sentimental value.'

'Was it the Edna Slaney book?'

'Well, in all honesty, I can't remember exactly. I showed him into the lounge and told him he'd probably have a better chance of finding whatever it was, but I do remember it had a yellow spine, so I'm thinking it probably was that one you were after.'

I nod. 'Yep, I'd say that was the mystery solved, Nan. Well done.'

'Well, it wasn't really great detective work, was it? More a case of my rusty old brain finally clicking into gear and remembering something.'

'I'd still like to read it. Would it be OK if I look on the internet? I want to get one from the same publisher, so it goes with the other ones we've got.'

'Course, love. Just don't get one that smells like it's been kept in a cellar. And don't pay £45 for it!'

I get the laptop. I check the right spelling of the publisher from the one I'm currently reading. The symbol is a hand holding a dagger and the publisher is called Pelikan House. I try some online bookshops. I find plenty of versions of the *The Owls of Grey Gardens* but not the one published by Pelikan House. I think about buying a different version, but then it just wouldn't look quite right with the others and I'd feel like I was messing up my mum and dad's collection. I try Google next. I type in: *Edna Slaney Owls Grey Gardens Pelikan House*. Nothing at all comes up for sale but there are some other links. The top one is a newspaper article: '*Incredibly rare: the most collectible books of the 20th century.'* I click on it to find a list of twenty books.

I'm still staring at the screen when Nan comes back with a cup of tea and some jammie dodgers.

'So, did you find one?'

I shake my head.

'What's up?' says Nan. I turn the laptop screen so that Nan can see it and point to number seven on the list. Nan puts her glasses on:

'Let's see, what's this you're showing me? *The Owls of Grey Gardens* – Edna Slaney (First edition Pelikan House 1935) Estimated Value: £28,000.'

Nan sits down heavily next to me and we both stare in silence for a few moments until Nan eventually says: 'And I thought £45 was a bit steep!'

CHAPTER THIRTEEN

There are strange goings on in Swingo Park today. A tall, skinny girl with sticky-up hair rocks back and forth on a swing made for someone at least two foot smaller than her. She lifts her feet high to stop them dragging along the ground. She appears to be talking to herself. A few feet away, concealed in a laurel bush, is a smaller girl wearing a camouflage jacket several sizes too big for her.

'Maybe he's not coming,' says Max.

'We've only been here four minutes,' whispers Lori.

'Feels longer than that,' Max replies.

'You have to be quite patient to be a detective.'

'I don't want to be a detective. I'm going to be a zoologist.'

'Well … patience is probably useful with animals too – I don't think they really understand punctuality, they can't even tell the time. Fang definitely can't, anyway.'

Max sighs. 'Mum always says I'm not very patient.'

'I think she might be right. Remember: softly softly, catchee monkey,' says Lori.

Max turns and looks directly at the speaking bush. 'What?'

'Softly, softly, catchee monkey,' says Lori and then adds, 'It's an expression.'

'No,' says Max simply, shaking her head. 'That's not an expression. It doesn't even make sense. What is "catchee"?'

'Well, I thought it was a well-known expression anyway. Nan often says it. But then again, she does say lots of things that I never hear anyone else say. I think it just means be patient or cautious or something like that.'

Max considers this. 'And the monkey bit?'

'I think it's just general advice if you're trying to catch a monkey. Might be useful for you when you're a zoologist.'

Max shakes her head. 'But we're not trying to catch a monkey. There aren't even any monkeys in Swingo Park.'

'Shhhhhhh!' hisses Lori. 'He's coming!'

Max watches as the boy she now knows is

101

Calum approaches. He sits on the bench next to the swings and scans the park. Max waits a moment and then goes over and sits on the other end of the bench.

'You're Calum, aren't you.'

He turns and looks at Max with some surprise. 'Who's asking?'

'I'm … I'm a friend of Taylor's.'

'A friend of Taylor's?' He sounds suspicious. 'Kids like him don't have any friends. Where is he anyway? He's supposed to be meeting me.'

'Actually … he sent me instead.'

Calum looks at her in disbelief. 'What? A girl?'

Max's annoyance makes her forget that she's nervous for a minute. 'Yeah, a girl! The name's Max, and I'm the girl whose phone you made him steal actually!'

He's up off the bench instantly and taking a step away. 'What? You're crazy. I don't know what you're talking about.'

Max regrets blurting it out. Lori wouldn't do that. She tries to remember the stupid monkey thing. 'Look, I'm not going to tell anyone. I just want to talk to you.'

But Calum starts to walk away. 'Well, that's

nice, but I don't want to talk to you, so bye. And you can tell Taylor he's in big trouble.'

Max bites her lip and looks over in the direction of the bush. She can vaguely make out Lori gesturing frantically, but Max doesn't know what it means.

'OK, fine,' she says, trying to think fast. 'I'm sure the police will understand.'

Calum hesitates. 'What do you mean police?'

'I'm sure they'll understand that you didn't really want to go along with all the fake muggings, didn't really want to force other kids to steal for you. Someone else made you do it, didn't they?'

He stares at her and she decides to keep going while he's listening.

'Only thing is, they might not understand why you didn't help catch that someone else when you had the chance.'

He looks at her. 'What do you mean "help catch"?'

'That's what I want to talk to you about. I've got a deal for you.'

He snorts. 'A deal?' But then he sits down quite suddenly. He speaks more quietly. 'You can't just catch Ryan.' Max tries to act cool and pretend she knew the name already. Calum carries on. 'He's careful and he's always on the look-out for snitches. Mainly he gets other people to do his dirty work anyway. He's got a whole crew of kids working for him.'

Max isn't quite sure what to say so she just nods and that seems to work.

'We each have our own patch. Mine's the park. I look out for kids that seem lonely or bored, kids wagging school, kids whose parents don't know or don't care where they are…'

Max's real feelings leak out again. 'And then you pretend to be their friend and trick them.'

Calum is defensive. 'Well, it's what I had done to me! Why shouldn't I? If I can get someone else to rip some phones then it means I don't have to do it.'

'And then Ryan sells the phones and you get a share of the money.'

Calum laughs for the first time. 'As if! Ryan makes out we're part of his team, his crew, but he never pays us anything. It's like the payment is not getting beaten up.'

'Why don't you help me then … get rid of him.'

He laughs again. 'Help you? Some little girl is going to catch Ryan all by herself! I don't think so and I'm definitely not being involved.'

'Who said I was on my own?'

'I don't see anybody else.'

'Oh, you wouldn't see anybody.' She tries to sound like Lori. 'This is strictly undercover.'

Max reaches for her pocket and holds up some of the long-range photos Lori took of Ryan and Calum. 'I'm just one part of a big surveillance operation. I'm working with professionals. They've got to use a kid to catch him – I'm just the bait.'

Calum stares at the photos. He bites his lip. 'What do you even want me to do?'

'Three things: first – I want you to get my phone back.'

He laughs again. 'Well, that's easy. I've still got it in my bag somewhere. No offence, but that phone was not worth the bother and definitely wasn't worth taking to Ryan. I got a right earful for that.' He rummages in his bag and finally finds the phone. 'Here, take it. It's a piece of junk anyway.'

'Secondly,' Max carries on despite finding Calum's remarks extremely rude, 'show me your phone.'

'What?'

'I just want to see it. Show me the phone you lent Taylor.'

Calum sighs and pulls the phone from his pocket. Max studies it closely.

'You see, that's we call a real phone,' says Calum. 'Maybe you should think about upgrading.'

'Maybe I am,' says Max.

'What was the third thing?'

'I want you to meet me here next Friday. Do like you did with Taylor. Lend me your phone and then go and tell Ryan that you've got someone else for him to mug.'

'Then what?'

'Then you don't need to know. You can't get blamed for something you don't even know.'

Calum looks uncertain. 'This is stupid. You've got your phone back. Why don't you just forget it? Ryan's not nice you know … and you're just some little girl.'

Max fixes him with a look. 'So? You're a boy and you're bigger than me but who's the one letting some bully push them around? Who's the one hanging around a little kid's playground every day? Yeah, I am a girl and I don't let bullies win.'

Calum rolls his eyes. 'Yeah, girl power, whatever.' He starts to walk away.

'See you Friday afternoon,' says Max a lot more confidently than she feels as she watches him go.

'Do you think he'll turn up?' she asks, as Lori emerges from the bush holding a half-eaten sandwich in one hand and her tape recorder in the other.

'We've got him on tape admitting what he does anyway. We can take it to the police.'

'We could stop now. I've got my phone back. We've got enough evidence against Calum but…'

'But what?'

'I hate what they've done to Taylor. He doesn't deserve it. No one deserves it and that Ryan is just going to keep on doing this until someone catches him red handed.'

Lori nods. 'He's the Mr Big of this investigation. Like I always say: you can't close a case without Mr Big.'

Max looks at her uncertainly. 'I've never heard you say that.'

Lori shrugs. 'Well, maybe that was the first time I said it out loud.'

CHAPTER FOURTEEN

Nan does not believe in eating meals in front of the telly. Snacks are permitted and that can, in exceptional circumstances, be stretched to include a sandwich. But an actual meal that comes on a plate and requires cutlery – never. She has a theory that you can only fully use one sense at a time. So: if you're watching, you're not tasting; or if you're speaking, you're not listening; or if you're fiddling with your buttons, you're not looking where you're going. So this evening when she hands me my tea on a tray and tells me to take it through to the living room, alarm bells start ringing:

'But Nan, we won't appreciate the meal,' I say.

'It's fine,' she replies.

'But surely we won't "savour the flavour".' This is something Nan likes to say a lot.

'No, honestly, it's OK. I deliberately made a very bland risotto, so there's not much flavour to savour anyway.'

I should have guessed that of course Hugo Smythe is to blame. It's a special episode of *Treasure Hunters* this evening where, according to the trailer that's been running all week: '*Hugo reveals his own personal treasures. The precious finds he just can't be parted from.*'

He'll also apparently be announcing some 'very special news'. This is the thing Nan is particularly excited about.

'This is it, Lori, love.' She said the first time she saw the trailer. 'This is the news I've been waiting for!'

'What's the announcement?' I asked. 'Oh, do you think he's going to start sharing all his money with the people he's taken stuff from?'

'For the hundredth time: he hasn't taken anything from anyone! He buys things. At a fair price.'

'But then he sells them for lots, lots more.'

'Well, that's just how the world works, love. No. That's not the announcement. I think it might be Open House!'

'What's open house?'

'It's when Hugo opens up his estate to the public.'

'His estate? What, like the Glebe estate? That's already open to the public.'

'No, not like the Glebe estate. That's a housing estate. I mean a stately home type estate. Hugo lives in a big house with lots of grounds.'

'Isn't that the sort of place where someone very, very rich would live, Nan?'

'Yes, but it's not like that. He bought it when it was a wreck and he's worked ever so hard to restore it. So on Open House there are guided tours of the property but, best of all, Hugo himself does valuations. You can take your own things for him to value. Honestly sometimes it's unbelievable. Someone takes in some old thing they've had in the attic for years and Hugo will tell them that it's actually worth thousands of pounds. You should see their faces! But the tickets go like hot cakes. I missed out last time. We've got to watch it live and, if that's what he's announcing, we're snapping up those tickets straight away.'

Nan has high hopes for a pair of candlesticks in the shape of monkeys that she found at the car boot this morning. We both got some good finds today, but I've no intention of getting mine valued by Hugo Smythe.

So here we are. Eating in front of the telly. Before he makes the mystery announcement we have to sit through Hugo telling us about his own collection of 'special finds'. He wonders around his massive house, pointing out rickety bits of furniture or bits and pieces he's taken from factories. The good thing is that because I'm not finding the programme as fascinating as Nan does, I'm able to fully concentrate on my sense of taste and I'm actually really enjoying my risotto.

'Look, love,' says Nan, 'He collects old books too.' I look up at the screen to see Hugo showing us around his 'library', which isn't a library where anyone can go and borrow books, but a massive room full of books just for him. It makes Mmum and Dad's collection look very small. 'Hmmm,' I say.

The programme seems to go on even longer than normal. Eventually it ends up with Hugo in his shop. You can see his staff in the background running around repairing and cleaning up old broken things so that they can be sold. I hadn't realised before but both Hugo's 'estate' and his shop are actually not far from New Heath – just out in the countryside a bit. Hugo finally makes the announcement that Nan has been waiting for. She was right all along – he's opening up 'Smythe Towers'. No sooner are the words out of his mouth than Nan is off to get her laptop to try and book tickets. I look at her tray left on the sofa. She's hardly eaten any of her risotto. People always say that watching too much telly causes obesity, but it actually seems quite a good way to lose weight. Though maybe that only works if you find what you're watching really, really exciting. Maybe normal telly doesn't suppress your appetite in the same way. I reach over for the remote control to turn the telly off when something catches my eye. *Treasure Hunters* is about to end, Hugo is saying goodbye and reminding us to buy tickets to come and walk around his house, but my attention is fixed at the back of the shot. A member of Hugo's staff is working on a laptop. Even sitting down it's clear that he's of above average height. He has distinctive curly hair and a telltale birthmark, shaped a bit like Australia, on his right cheek. I've stopped noticing how delicious the risotto is.

After I've helped Nan wash and put away the dishes, I go up to my office and sit and think for a while. I say office, but technically it's my bedroom and I'd have to admit that my bedroom is a pretty long way from anyone's idea of a private eye's office. It's painted yellow for a start and covered with hand-painted stars and rainbows and strange mythical creatures. My mum and dad decorated the room when they found out I was on the way and it's definitely an excellent room for a baby, maybe even a very small child. It's less good for a professional detective. Nan's told me I can redecorate, but I don't like the idea of painting over my parents' work, I think it might feel like I was trying to erase them. So instead I've just tried to integrate professional office supplies into the room as best as I can. I have a flip chart, obviously, a desk calendar, a small filing cabinet, I also happen to have the world's best chair. It's black and padded and not only swivels round and round but also goes up and down when you pull a lever. The overall effect though is still not quite right – basically I have an office in a nursery. To be honest, it would feel a bit awkward interviewing clients here, but luckily as I've yet to ever have an actual, real-life client, it hasn't been a problem.

I sit in my chair and think. Spinning slowly in

my deluxe swivel chair is one of the very best things for thinking. If a problem is really tricky then sometimes I might go further still, open the drawer in my desk, get out my deerstalker and put that on as well. Nan bought me the hat because (a) Sherlock Holmes always wore a deerstalker and she knows how much I admire Sherlock Holmes and (b) she thinks the world would just be a better place in general if everyone wore hats. I don't wear the deerstalker out of the house. Nan is a very confident hat-wearer. She never thinks for a second that she might look a bit crazy, even on her sombrero days. I don't seem to have inherited her confidence though and so I'm a clandestine hat wearer – strictly indoors only (unless the hat is part of a disguise, in which case, anything goes).

My top-secret notebook is mainly filled with one-off suspicious incidents that don't seem to lead anywhere. Sometimes though another thing happens that could be connected. And sometimes maybe another thing too. And sometimes all these things that may or may not be connected and that may or may not be suspicious start to float up out of my notebook and lodge in my brain. I can't fully explain except to say it's a bit like a fog that fills my head. That's when I put on my deerstalker, rotate slowly in my chair and think. I'm waiting for the fog to lift.

Today it takes twenty-three minutes. I go downstairs to the study and pull an enormous plastic crate out of the cupboard. I take off the lid and survey the contents. The crate contains all the old printed photos that Mum and Dad left behind. Some are in albums, some in old shoeboxes, some in frames. At the bottom of the crate are lots of slippery, brown strips of plastic which Nan has explained are negatives. I start taking things out and piling them on the floor around me. I'm looking for some specific photos that I've seen before, but can't remember exactly where. I can't even remember if they were loose or in an album. There's nothing for it but to go through everything. It's not quite as daunting as it first seems. Some boxes are obviously from before Mum and Dad met, so there are entire boxes just of Mum and her friends and family and others of Dad's side. The ones I'm looking for are of my dad, so I know I can ignore the ones of my mum, but for some reason I keep forgetting this and spend ages looking through photos of her when she was young. I find one of her around my age. She has longer hair than I have now and she's wearing some kind of tracksuit, but her face looks like mine. Her mouth is open as if she's in the middle of speaking and I keep looking and looking and imagining what she might be saying. I decide to keep the photo in my room.

I finally find what I'm looking for: Dad's school photos. He has a whole album of school stuff – posed individual portraits, him with the football team, him in class photos, even whole school photos. It's weird to watch him get older as the album goes on. At the beginning he looks like boys in my class and then gradually his face begins to change, his chin and nose get bigger, his eyes change shape, lots of spots come and then go, his hair gets worse and worse. By the end of the album he kind of looks like the grown-up version of himself, but with really crazy spiky hair. I get my magnifying glass and go carefully through all the group shots – every team, class and whole school photo. It takes a long time to check all of them thoroughly, but I make sure I study every single face. Some boys are taller than others, some have very curly hair, they come in all shapes and sizes but not a single boy in the entire school has a distinctive birthmark covering their right cheek.

CHAPTER FIFTEEN

'I'm not sure the camouflage is necessary; you're invisible in there anyway,' says Max to the nearby bush.

'The camouflage is why I'm invisible,' answers the bush.

The girls are back in Swingo Park. Max is trying to process everything that Lori has been telling her.

'So you think Gordon is an imposter?'

'Yes,' says Lori's voice from the bush. 'Exactly.'

'Why would he lie about being friends with your dad?'

'To fool Nan and steal the book that's worth loads of money.'

'Right. But if he wasn't really friends with your dad, how did he know he had the book?'

'Probably from the auction house. I've been thinking about it. Nan says Dad used to get his books at auctions – and they're public places, you can see who's bidding on what and who wins.

Maybe Gordon missed out on the book at auction for some reason but saw Dad get it. Maybe he didn't even know how valuable it was at that point but found out later. The thing is when my mum and dad died it was in the local paper. Nan has the cutting. So I reckon Gordon must have seen that and then seen an opportunity to get his hands on the book.'

Max doesn't ask about the newspaper article. She's never asked how Lori's parents died. If Lori decides one day she wants to tell her then Max will be ready to listen, but until then Max thinks it's not her business. She thinks instead of Gordon Trent tricking Lori's nan and it makes her angry.

'How could someone do that? Who could lie to your nan about a thing like that? At a time like that? And just for a book!'

Lori seems unsurprised. 'Hobbies seem quite dangerous in detective books, especially collecting things. Crime stories are full of obsessive collectors. People kill to get hold of rare things all the time. I read one once where a man killed eight people just to get hold of a particular orchid! Justice always catches up with them in the end.'

'But you can't prove any of this. What are you going to do?'

'I'm working on it.'

Lori goes quiet and Max gets another chunk of pineapple rock from her pocket. Max has yet to find a sweet she doesn't like, but she has a particular affection for acidic, tangy candy. She's tried all the gimmicky, pretend toxic, bitter sweets but she favours the old-fashioned classics: pineapple rock, pear drops, acid drops. Mr Meacham of course knows Max's confectionery preferences and is always on the look-out for newer, ever more zingy options for her to try. The pineapple rock she has today is from a new supplier and Mr Meacham has given Max a giant bag for free in exchange for feedback. The rock makes Max's tongue feel fuzzy, like when she eats rhubarb. She has four chunks in her mouth right now and it feels as if her entire head is fizzing. Sour sweets are exactly what tense situations require.

She sees Calum approaching and coughs to alert Lori. She feels both relieved and nervous at the same time. When he gets to the bench he reaches in his pocket and pulls out a phone with a large screen.

'Take this. Ryan will come and find you.'

Max nods, partly because speaking is difficult with a mouth full of pineapple rock.

Calum looks at her and sniffs. 'I don't know what your plan is but I'm warning you – you better leave me out of it … or else.'

Max wants to tell him that she's not scared of his threats, she wants to say something clever that shuts him up, but her teeth seem to have stuck together, so she settles for a shrug.

Calum gives her one last stare and then slinks away.

Max heads over to the laurel bush. She and Lori check the model carefully. 'Nice work,' whispers Lori. 'You played it cool.'

'Argleglarkzed,' says Max.

'What?'

Max finally manages to swallow some sweets. 'I said, "This rock's amazing."' She returns to the bench and Lori calls over, 'Nan says sweets are the worst things for your teeth.'

'Everyone says that.'

'Maybe everyone is right.'

'I know they're right. It's obvious – sweets are bad for your teeth. Everyone just assumes.'

There's a pause and then Lori finally asks, 'Assumes what?'

'Assumes it's a problem.'

'Isn't it?'

'Haven't they heard of false teeth? I mean things have moved on. It's not the middle ages. If I lose my teeth I'm not going to die – I'll get some plastic ones, probably be better. Then I can eat whatever sweets I like and when someone says "Be careful – they'll make your teeth fall out," I can turn around and say, "Don't worry! They already have!" and show them my PVC dentures. Could even get gold ones if I was rich.'

The bush is silent for a moment and then says, 'I never thought of it like that.'

Max shakes her head. 'No, well, no one ever does, except me and Mr Meacham. He's already got false teeth. He says it's the best thing that ever happened to him.'

'Right,' says Lori. 'Did you know Mr Meacham and Nan are going out together next week?'

'Out? Where?'

'I don't know. Nan just said Mr Meacham phoned and said he'd like to take her "out".'

'I think he likes your nan. He was going on about her to me before. Do you mind?'

Lori thinks. 'No, I don't mind. I like people to like Nan. It's just a bit mysterious, isn't it? "Out"?'

Max nods. 'I think it's just what people do. It's probably OK.'

'Uh-oh,' says Lori.

'What?' says Max.

'I think I see him.'

'Mr Meacham?'

'No!' hisses Lori, 'Ryan!'

Max pretends to look down at the phone in her hand, but sneakily peeks up to scan the park. She sees a man on a bike heading directly towards the playground. Her heart starts racing. She suddenly feels that this is a bad idea. She knows she is about to be mugged and the fact that she knows it's going to happen doesn't make it any less scary. Why is it only now that she remembers Taylor mentioning a knife? She imagines a blade coming towards her, slashing at her clothes. She wants to run but she doesn't. She forces herself to sit still and remember scary moments from the past. She has a memory of her mum holding her tight while strangers hammered on the front door looking for her dad. She puts another piece of pineapple rock in her mouth and sucks furiously. She swallows her fear. She takes a deep breath, hears the squeak of bike brakes and feels a shadow fall across her.

'Nice phone,' says the voice. She looks up and sees Ryan's face up close. He's quite baby-faced but has stubble on his chin and spots across his nose. She almost hands him the phone straight away, but remembers that she has a part to play.

'Oh, thanks,' she says.

'It wasn't a compliment. Hand it over.'

'What?'

'Are you stupid or deaf? Hand over the phone.'

'But … it's not mine. I'm looking after it for a friend.'

'You can either give it to me or…' He lifts his top slightly to show a knife handle sticking out of his joggers. '…I'll take it. Makes no difference to me.'

Max bites her lip and then slowly passes the phone over. Ryan snatches it, shoves it in his back pocket and cycles off at speed.

Max breathes out heavily.

'It *is* a nice phone?' says the bush. Lori

emerges holding the same model. 'Amazing quality video.'

Max looks up. 'Do you think you got it all? Did you get the knife?'

'Yeah. It was all really clear. No wonder this model costs such a lot of money.'

'I still can't believe you found the same type.'

'It wasn't hard, there are literally tons of dead phones at the car boot.'

They gather their things quickly and start running towards the gate.

'Come on. Let's get this to the police before he notices.' Max runs ahead, a mixture of adrenaline and sugar racing around her body. She feels as if she could fly.

CHAPTER SIXTEEN

'I hope you understand that this was not a sensible thing to do. You exposed yourselves to very considerable danger. You, Max, should have told your teacher when your phone went missing instead of trying to take the law into your own hands.'

I'm beginning to think that Sergeant Craig Ashworth is a bit ungrateful. I mean, I didn't expect a medal for cracking the mobile phone theft ring (well, maybe I did, but I know that only happens in books), but I didn't think we'd get told off. Max looks bored. She's staring off into space while Sergeant Craig Ashworth goes on and on, I think she might be running through the marsupial factfile in her head.

It turns out that reporting crime is not as easy as I thought. After we left the park we ran as fast as we could all the way to the local police station and that's when we found out it was closed. I didn't believe it at first. I kept walking around the outside looking for an open door. I just didn't know that police stations closed. I mean hospitals don't close, do they? Petrol stations don't close. Even the Select and Save on New Heath High Street is open twenty-four hours for anyone who wants to buy crisps or those big bottles of weird blue pop they sell in there. Eventually Max spotted a sign saying that the nearest station open to the public was in the city centre and even that had limited opening hours! You never see this on telly. On TV cop shows there's always a waiting room filled with people eager to share vital clues or confess to unsolved crimes. There's usually a drunk person too, shouting a lot, I'm not sure why. Sometimes I worry about just how accurate television is.

Now we're here in the central police station and Nan's here with us because they said we needed an adult. Nan looked shocked when she saw the video footage and heard what we'd been up to. Nan doesn't really get angry, but she looks quite cross now. I'm worried that I might be in for a telling off from her as soon as Detective Craig Ashworth finishes his go first.

'By putting yourselves at risk like this, you could have become victims of crime and made the situation a lot worse.'

Nan sighs. 'But they didn't, did they?'

Detective Craig Ashworth looks at her and blinks. 'I'm sorry?'

'They didn't become victims of crime or make the situation worse. Instead they've handed you very clear evidence to arrest this nasty piece of work Ryan and to help lads like Calum and Taylor who've been trapped by him.'

'Be that as it may, I'm sure you'll agree that it's better if the police deal with dangerous individuals like this.'

'Well, that's where you're wrong. I don't agree at all.' says Nan. 'What have the police done about him so far? Sounds like he's been getting away with this scot free for goodness knows how long. How many poor lads has he got out breaking the law for him? What were you doing about him?'

'Mrs Southwell, what the girls did was dangerous.'

'And I'm going to be talking to them about that, don't you worry, but I don't believe for a second that you were going to put a stop to this anytime soon and neither do the girls. Just because they're eleven doesn't mean they're stupid and you're not giving a very good impression of the police by talking to them as if they were.'

Detective Craig Ashworth takes his glasses off and rubs his eyes. He puts his glasses on the table and looks at Max and me.

'Girls, what you did was dangerous.' He holds up his hand to Nan to allow him to finish. 'But it was also brave and clever. Forgive me for focusing on the danger first, but I'm a police officer and that's what I do. We have some awareness of Ryan as a known associate of criminals but, in all honesty, we didn't know anything about this phone theft racket. You've given us enough evidence to arrest Ryan and that in turn might lead to more information about a wider criminal network operating in the area.' He pauses and then adds. 'Congratulations, you did a good job.'

Max speaks for the first time. 'What about Taylor? Is he going to get into trouble?'

'I would consider Taylor to be another victim in this case. I'll be talking to him and this other boy, Calum, and trying to get information on any other children caught up in this but we won't be looking to prosecute. We'll also make it crystal clear to Ryan that we are keeping a very close eye on the boys he formerly controlled and ensuring their safety.'

He sits back and gives a little smile. 'So, I take it you both fancy careers in the police when you grow up?'

Max looks at him as if he's mad.

'No. Last thing I want to do. I'm going to be a zoologist,' she says.

'Oh, I see,' says Detective Ashworth looking rather deflated. He turns to me. 'What about you though? You're the keen evidence collector, I bet you fancy the police.'

I think for a moment and then shake my head. 'It was an option in the past,' I say, 'but I've decided to devote myself to private detective work. This business of closing police stations has made my mind up. It's just not professional. Private detectives are always on call. Crime doesn't sleep you know.'

CHAPTER SEVENTEEN

The wind works in strange ways on the Glebe estate. Max's mum says it's because of the tower blocks. Apparently people who live on the top floors can feel the blocks swaying slightly on really windy days. That makes some sense to Max, but what she doesn't understand is the way that even at ground level the wind can be so fierce and unpredictable. Sometimes she turns a corner and a massive gust hits her so hard she can't move forward. It's like a giant invisible hand pushing her back to where she's come from. The wind does weird things to the litter as well. There's always loads of litter on the Glebe, not because people are any messier there than anywhere else, but because the wind blows it out of the bins. Max is fascinated by the patterns it makes. Some areas are totally bare, because the wind's blasted every scrap away. In other places there are neat lines of litter all down one side where fences and walls and bushes have acted as traps and captured every passing crisp packet and tissue. Max's favourite litter phenomenon though is the garbage twisters – cyclones of airborne debris spinning round and round, sometimes towering so high in the sky she can see them outside her eighth-floor window. She doesn't know why but she finds them weirdly exciting. Sometimes if there's no one to see her, she even chases them, shouting and screaming into the roar of the wind as she does. Today she's sitting on the bollards outside the back door of the block talking to Taylor when one starts up.

'Look!' she says.

'Oh no!' says Taylor putting his hood up. 'Whirlwind! Let's get inside.'

'It's only litter, it's not going to hurt you,' Max shouts over the noise of the wind.

'That's what you think. I got a chip paper wrapped round my head last week and couldn't see where I was going and walked into a lamp post.'

'Do you ever think you might be a bit unlucky?' Max calls, but the tornado dies as quickly as it started and all is quiet again.

Taylor takes his hood down. 'I do actually. All the time.'

They're both quiet for a moment and then Max says, 'At least you can go to Swingo Park again now on Friday afternoons.'

Taylor's face brightens. 'I might not have to.'

'Has your mum given you a key?'

'No. No chance of that happening.'

'Have you found somewhere else to go?'

'Kind of. Actually, it was Mr Probert's idea.'

'Probert?'

'The police spoke to him, you know about what happened at school, the phone stuff. Then he spoke to me.'

'Let me guess: "Now Taylor, you won't get away with that kind of thing in the real world." That's what he said, I bet you a million pounds.'

'You owe me a million pounds.'

'What? But he went on about when he was in business though, yeah?'

'Not really. He asked me loads of questions about home, about my mum, that kind of thing. Did you know he was brought up in foster care?'

'No.'

'Yeah, he told me about it. He was bullied at school for a while as well.'

Max thinks for a minute and then nods. 'Do

133

you remember that time Tyrone was mean about you living on the Glebe? Most teachers would have just told him to be quiet, but Mr Probert kicked him out of the class. I thought that was good.'

'Yeah.'

'I can't imagine Mr Probert being bullied.'

'He was OK in the end. He had this one foster mum who was brilliant. She was always telling him he could achieve anything.'

'That's good,' Max says and then falls quiet. She gets the impression that Taylor's mum isn't the type to say stuff like that.

'Anyway,' says Taylor, 'he's decided he's going to start up a club on Friday afternoons for anyone who wants to join.'

'There's already an after-school club on Fridays.'

'I know, but he says this is different. It'll be free for one thing. It's just something he wants to do.'

'What kind of club?'

'He wants us to set up a kids' news channel, you know, online. Like a vlog, but about stuff that happens in New Heath, run by local kids.'

Max repeats the word 'Vlog' just because she likes the feel of it in her mouth.

Taylor carries on. 'He's got loads of experience of telly. He spent years working on one of those shopping channels. He used to produce the programmes. Jewellery was his speciality.'

Max looks at him. 'What? That was the "business" he was in? Those programmes where you just look at some woman's ear and a voice tells you how much her earrings are?'

'Yeah.'

'Wow. Wait till I tell Lori, she's been trying to work out his past for ages.'

'Guess what he wants to call the news site?'

'What?'

'*The real world.*'

Max looks at Taylor and they both laugh.

CHAPTER EIGHTEEN

Today is the day that Nan has been waiting for. She set the alarm for 5.30 and we're out of the house, walking to the bus stop by 6am. Although Smythe Towers is not that far from New Heath, it's not very easy to get to on public transport. This is one of the problems with the countryside – they don't really have buses out there. I don't know how people get around if they can't drive. I guess they ride horses or tractors, cows possibly, I'm not sure. The truth is I've never really been to the countryside. I mean car boot sales are often in fields, but they're never properly out in the middle of nowhere and there's always a bus. Pretty much everything I know about the countryside has come from watching detective programmes on the telly. More specifically detective programmes on the telly on a Sunday night because that's when people like watching murders either in the olden days or in the countryside. Here's what I've learned about the countryside:

1. Very high concentration of hats and dogs.
2. Everyone is white.
3. Farmers are generally unfriendly.
4. No buses, big shops or retail parks.
5. No litter.
6. High murder rate.

It's two buses and a long walk to get to Smythe Towers. We arrive at 7.30am and by the look of the overflow car parks there are already hundreds and hundreds of people here ahead of us. Nan and I join a queue. A jolly woman with a clipboard is checking everyone. If you only have one or two items you can join another, faster queue. Nan has brought the pair of candlesticks she found at the car boot and I've asked her to bring one of our vintage Edna Slaney books too for research purposes. The woman with the clipboard gets to us.

'Ah? Now you have three items so I'm sorry it's a bit of a long wait in this queue for you.' She's very smiley about it.

'But we only have two items,' I say.

'Oh dear, someone's not top of the class at maths, are they?' She laughs. She is the poshest person I've ever met in real life. 'One, two candlesticks plus a book, that makes three!' And with that she moves on to the people behind us.

'But the candlesticks are a pair,' I say to Nan. 'He's not going to value them separately, is he?'

'Don't worry, love,' says Nan. 'It's just because she's got a clipboard. Sends people power mad.'

Nan doesn't mind waiting in the queue. We are surrounded by people wearing a wide variety of hats, all gossiping excitedly about Hugo Smythe. It is Nan heaven. We learn that Hugo doesn't do all the valuations – he has a team of specialists helping out. He will do some, so it's a bit of a lottery and there is a lot of talk about how best to maximise your chances of getting to meet him. The woman in front who has brought a rickety old milking stool is jealous of our Edna Slaney.

'Oh, aren't you clever? Books are really Hugo's passion so I'll bet he'll be doing all the book valuations.' Nan is delighted with this news and squeezes my hand. 'Well done, Lori.'

It's only when we are near the front of the line that I get to see into the grounds of Smythe Towers properly. Little tents are dotted around the vast lawn and threading between the tents are queues and queues of people. It turns out that the queue we've been in for the last hour is just a queue to get tickets to join other queues. We take our tickets and join the back of the 'Rare Books and Maps' line. Even Nan sighs when she sees how many people are ahead of us.

'I'm sorry, love. I didn't think there would be so much waiting. They never show this on the telly.'

'It's OK, Nan.' I clutch the book in my hands. 'I can always re-read this if I get bored.'

'I'll get the flask out,' says Nan.

She pours us both a cup of tea.

'So, did you have a nice time with Mr Meacham yesterday?' I ask.

'Oh yes. I haven't had a chance to talk to you about it!'

'Where did you go?'

'He took me to a lovely garden centre.'

'A garden centre?' I'm a bit disappointed by this. 'Out' had sounded a lot more mysterious.

'Yes, it was smashing. He's got a loyalty card so we got free tea and cake. You get that once a month with the card and you also get twenty per cent off purchases over fifty pounds and ten per cent off purchases under fifty pounds.'

Loyalty cards are one of Nan's specialist subjects. She has hundreds of them. Whatever shop we're in she always takes ages at the till looking for the right one in her enormous leopard-print purse.

'Is Mr Meacham into loyalty cards, too?' I ask.

'Yes, we had a good old chin wag about which ones were the best. He's got a system; he was telling me all about it. Different shops on different days of the week depending on which ones are offering double points, it's quite complicated but very clever.'

'Right.'

'Yes, I have to say, we got on like a house on fire.'

This is another of Nan's expressions that I find confusing. I can't see anything friendly about a burning building.

'Guess what he asked me?' she says.

I have a sudden worry that Mr Meacham might have asked Nan to marry him. I like Mr Meacham but it seems too soon.

'What?' I say.

'He's asked me if I want to combine our supermarket points and get some free cinema tickets!' She beams at me. 'I said yes!'

After an hour and a half, we are nearing the front of the line. We can finally see inside the tent and Nan gives a delighted gasp.

'Oh Lori, look! It's Hugo – we're actually going to meet him!'

I'm glad too. I look around for any sign of Gordon. I'm sure he's here somewhere.

'Do you think we'll be on the telly?' I ask Nan.

'I don't know. They can't film all of us, can they? The programme would go on for days. You've got your phone though, haven't you? Will you video it all for us?'

'Yep. I've got it. The video is a bit rubbish, but I'll make sure I record you anyway.'

Hugo isn't at all like he is on the telly. On T*reasure Hunters* he's always very excited about everything he finds and he loves chatting to people. In real life he looks a bit bored. He doesn't spend much time on the valuations and doesn't seem very impressed with any of the books or maps that are brought to him. He also seems to need a lot of breaks. After about every four people he stops for a cigarette or to eat one from a seemingly never-ending supply of sausage rolls and chat to the woman with the clipboard. Nan gets quieter and quieter the longer we wait. At first I think it's excitement or nerves but then I notice that she has the look in her eyes. It was the same look she had just before she ticked off Sergeant Craig Ashworth. It's Nan's steely glare.

'Are you OK, Nan?' I ask.

'Did you see that? He was just rude to that old gentleman. The man was trying to tell him how his book had been passed down the family. Hugo didn't even look him in the eye. He actually interrupted him to tell him it was worth nothing!'

I'm wondering what to say to this when quite suddenly we're at the front of the queue. We sit down across the table from Hugo Smythe. He smells of cigarette smoke with a faint whiff of sausage. I set my phone to video and put the book on the table. It's the first time since we've entered the tent that I see a flicker of interest in his eyes. He reaches out for the book.

'Ah ah,' says Nan, quickly sliding the book out of his reach.

He looks up at her. 'What are you doing?' he says.

'I don't know where you're from,' smiles Nan sweetly. 'But where I live it's polite to greet people on first meeting, particularly people who have been queuing patiently all day to meet you, but leaving that aside, I've seen you've been stuffing yourself with sausage rolls all morning and I have no intention of letting you touch this book until you've gone and washed your hands.'

Hugo looks shocked. He turns to the woman with the clipboard. She shrugs and he pushes his chair back in search of a sink. I glance behind me to see how annoyed the people in the queue are at the extra delay but to my surprise there is a little outburst of applause and mutterings of 'Well done' and 'Well said!' to Nan. When Hugo returns, he gives Nan a fake smile. 'May I?' He says gesturing to the book. Nan nods and he picks it up and starts checking it very thoroughly. He takes a long time. At one point he calls clipboard lady over and whispers something in her ear. She nods and disappears. Eventually he pushes the book back across the table to Nan.

'Well, thanks for bringing this in today. I'm sorry to say it's worth very little. Maybe ten pounds if you're lucky.'

Nan looks at me and gives a little shrug. 'Never mind, eh, love?'

'It's OK, Nan,' I say.

'Thank you for that,' says Nan to Hugo Smythe. She's never impolite even when she's cross. 'Come on, let's get out of here,' she says to me. I grab the book and we leave.

Outside the marquee Nan looks deflated. 'I can't be bothered with the candlesticks now,' she says. 'What a horrible man he turned out to be. About as much charm as a stubbed toe. Well I certainly won't be watching *Treasure Hunters* anymore anyway.'

I never really liked Hugo but I feel sad for Nan. She really loved that programme. He could at least have carried on pretending to be nice for the people who'd queued up for so long. I hope she doesn't give up on the car boots; it'd be a shame if Hugo Smythe ruined that bit of fun for Nan forever.

'Do you know what I really fancy?' she says.

'No,' I say.

'A nice chicken balti! I could murder one right now.'

'With peshwari naan!' I say.

'Yes! Exactly. Let's get back to civilisation, shall we, and call in at Diwan before it closes?'

It's then that I see him walking towards us.

'Well, I never! Hello again!' says Gordon Trent. He's much smilier today. I do my best to make my face neutral. I don't want him to guess that I suspect anything at this stage.

'Oh hello, love,' says Nan. 'What a coincidence bumping into you again.'

'Isn't it?' He nods. 'I hope you don't mind, but I was queuing in books and maps too and I couldn't help overhear your valuation.'

'Well, there wasn't much to hear, was there?' says Nan.

'Look, I know he said it's not worth much, but the thing is, that book actually is worth something to me. As you know I have another in that publisher's series and they have some sentimental value for me. I wonder, would you accept twenty pounds for it?'

'Well, that's twice what he said it's worth, so I appreciate the offer, but Lori's not actually interested in selling, are you, love?'

'Oh, I am,' I say and turn to Gordon. 'Twenty pounds would be great, thanks. It's OK, Nan, just think of all the sweeties I can buy.' Nan gives me a strange look as Gordon hands over the money.

Once he has the book, I take my camera out again and take a quick snap.

He turns sharply. 'What's that for?' he says.

'Oh, just a souvenir of today. I've taken photos and videos of everything, haven't I, Nan? Never visited a TV show before, it's so exciting!'

He looks uncertain for a minute and then shrugs. 'OK. Well, I'd best be off. Thanks again.'

Nan waits till he's out of earshot and then turns to me.

'"Just think of all the sweeties I can buy"? You don't even like sweets!'

'I know.'

'And you wanted to get the whole set of those books and now you've let one go.'

'I know,' I say again.

Nan narrows her eyes in her classic interrogating detective-sergeant manner. 'You're up to something, Lori Mason! I thought I made it very clear after the incident at the police station the other day that I didn't want any more secrets or surprises.'

'I know,' I say for the third time, grinning. 'Come on, Nan, I'll fill you in on the bus.'

CHAPTER NINETEEN

They've only been off the bus for ten minutes and Max has already decided that she loves the countryside. She loves how much sky you can see. She loves how many birds you can hear. She even loves the smell. Fang is excited too. He tugs on the lead as they turn into the long drive up to *Salvaged Treasure*, Hugo Smythe's showroom.

Taylor sneezes for the fourth time since they got off the bus and Lori hands him a tissue.

'Thanks. I think I caught a cold on the bus,' he says.

'It's probably hay fever,' says Lori. 'There's all stuff in the air in the countryside. Invisible but harmful.'

Taylor looks around suspiciously.

'It's just pollen,' says Max. 'It's better than breathing in car fumes.' Lori and Taylor both look dubious.

'I'm going to let Fang off the lead for a bit. He needs a run around before we go in.'

'I'm not sure it was a good idea to bring the dog,' says Lori. 'We're on a mission. He's not fully trained. It's not really professional.'

Max pats him. 'Hey! He can hear you know. It's not his fault your nan had a dental appointment. Anyway, he is trained. Look at this.' She picks up a stick and throws it as far as she can. Fang runs in the opposite direction. 'Have you ever seen a cleverer dog?' Max asks delightedly.

'Erm…' says Lori.

Salvaged Treasure is located in a converted barn at Smythe Towers. Inside, the shop is as big as a warehouse with enormous old tables and benches dotted about, covered with a seemingly random assortment of old things. Max spots a Victorian carousel horse, an old-fashioned telephone box, an enormous model of a whale.

'What is this place?' says Taylor.

'It's just a shop,' says Lori.

'Filled with creepy things,' says Max. 'Still – at least dogs are allowed.'

'It's the countryside,' says Lori. 'I think they prefer dogs to people.'

'Who buys this stuff?' says Max, looking around.

'I don't know,' says Lori. 'People like them?' She points to a couple over in the corner closely examining an incredibly big and rusty-looking bucket. 'Why are they wearing sunglasses indoors? Do you think they're undercover detectives?'

'I think they're just rich,' says Max.

They wander around until they find what they've been looking for at the back of the shop. A glass case filled with old books and prints. Taylor gets out his mini-cam and starts recording.

'There it is!' says Lori, pointing to the Edna Slaney book she sold to Gordon Trent the previous week. The price label next to the book says £250. Taylor zooms in.

Max whistles. 'That's a lot of money.'

'It's not really worth that much,' says Lori. 'It said about £150 on the internet. Hugo just bumps the price up. That whole Pelikan House series of Edna Slaney novels is quite rare but the super valuable one was *The Owls of Grey Gardens* – that's the one I can never get back.'

Max notices a very thin woman start heading directly towards them.

'Uh-oh,' says Lori. 'It's clipboard woman.'

Taylor takes a few steps back behind a stuffed polar bear to avoid her attention but carries on filming discreetly.

'Who?' says Max, but the woman is already in front of them, with a worried look on her face.

'Excuse me, girls. Where is your adult?'

Lori and Max look at each other and then look at the woman uncomprehendingly.

'Children must be accompanied by an adult,' she says, pointing to a sign on the wall. She looks disapprovingly from Lori to Max to Fang without noticing Taylor. 'A grown-up,' she adds, as if they don't understand the word adult.

Max glances at Lori and then says, 'My father is parking his car at the moment. We're interested in buying this book.' She taps on the glass. 'Can you open the case so we can look at it, please?'

'Look at it?'

'Yes. We want to check it's the right one.'

'Oh,' the woman says with a smirk. 'I suppose you're a specialist in rare books, are you?'

'No, I'm not...'

'Well, in that case I think we'll wait until your father arrives before we start pawing the book, shall we?'

'I'm not a specialist in rare books, but my father's assistant here is.' Max nudges Lori and Clipboard Lady's eyes widen. 'Oh really?' She gives Lori a fake smile. 'Perhaps you'd like to tell me something about it. I always love to learn from an expert.'

Lori is frozen then Max clears her throat and she's jolted into speaking. 'Well, this is a relatively rare Edna Slaney first edition, published in 1938. Of interest mainly to collectors. One of a set of eight Slaney novels published by Pelikan House – each distinguished by a different-coloured spine.'

Clipboard Lady blinks.

Max grins. 'Now could we hurry it along, please? Daddy doesn't like to be kept waiting.' The woman fumbles with her keys and opens the case. She gently lays the book on a table. Lori examines it closely and then calls over to Taylor. He comes over to get some close ups.

'Oh!' says Clipboard Woman when she sees Taylor. 'Another one. Goodness! Where are you all coming from? Excuse me, young man, but I didn't say anything about photographing the book!' She turns to Max. 'Are you sure your father is coming? He's taking an awfully long time to park a car.'

At that moment, a door at the side of the shop opens. Through the door the main house is visible, a tiled floor leads off into the distance. Two men walk into the shop space, deep in conversation. Max vaguely recognises Hugo Smythe from the telly, she guesses that the other man with the mark on his face is Gordon.

'Hells bells, Tiffany!' exclaims Hugo. 'Am I getting older or are the punters getting younger? Ha ha! I'm not sure we should be allowing kids to touch the rare books, though.'

'It's alright, darling, the father's on his way. He's a collector apparently.'

'My father?' says Max. 'The only things my dad ever collected were bits of tin foil to make into a really big tin foil ball, but he gave that up eventually.'

Tiffany's face darkens. 'Right then, you jokers. I think it's time you left.'

She starts making ineffective shooing motions at the three of them, but stops when Fang starts growling. Taylor captures the moment when the man with the birthmark on his face notices Lori and tries to retreat back to the door. Lori calls out to him, 'Hello, Gordon. I thought this book had sentimental value to you.'

Gordon turns around and does a bad job of pretending to be surprised. 'Oh, hi there. We must stop bumping into each other like this!' He laughs nervously and then stops abruptly. 'Sorry, which book are you talking about?'

'This book!' says Lori, holding it up.

'Oh!' he says 'Wow. Isn't that a copy of the very same book I bought off you last week? What an incredible coincidence!'

'That's right,' says Lori, turning to Hugo Smythe. 'The same book that you told my nan was worth ten pounds at most. Now it's for sale in your shop for £250.'

Hugo laughs. 'Ah – that's where I recognise you from. Yes, I remember, you were with that bad-tempered old lady, weren't you?' He pulls a face. 'Oh dear, is granny a bit cantankerous? I bet she's always showing you up, isn't she?' Max steals a glance at Lori and notices a very set look in her eyes. Hugo carries on, oblivious. 'Now, as I remember, after causing a bit of a scene, your dear granny produced a very inferior copy of a Slaney novel to be valued. It was a later publication and, if anything, the valuation I gave her was generous. Sorry to say it, sweetheart, but you're no expert and just because this looks a bit like some other book it doesn't mean it is. Now I think we'd better get that back in the case before you make it dirty.'

Lori holds on to the book. 'You're right, I'm not really an expert but you don't have to be an expert to know it's a first edition because it says it right here for anyone to see.' She points to the publication information at the front of the book and holds it out for Taylor to capture. 'What's less noticeable is on the very last page.' She flicks forward to show them. 'This funny, indented mark, here.' She holds it up and both Hugo and the other man squint to see. 'Can you see, it says J&SM?'

Hugo mutters to Gordon. 'What the hell is that?'

'It's an embossed stamp belonging to my mum and dad,' says Lori. 'Jim and Sylvie Mason. They died ten years ago, and one day soon after, Gordon visited saying he was an old friend of my dad's. He wanted to pay his respects to my nan and asked very politely if he could take back a book my dad had borrowed.'

'Well, that's terribly sad about your ma and pa, I'm sure, but I don't know what this has got to do with me,' says Hugo.

Lori carries on as if she hasn't heard. 'Since then I've made three important discoveries.' She counts out on her fingers. 'One: how much the book was worth. Two: that Gordon was a liar and had never been a friend of my dad's. Three: that Gordon works for you.'

She takes a step closer to Hugo. Max notices how, unlike most people, Lori's voice gets quieter rather than louder when she's angry.

'At some point, you found out how much that version of *The Owls of Grey Gardens* was really worth. Gordon here remembered my dad getting it at auction and you couldn't bear to think that someone else had it. But your lucky day came – you read about my parents' deaths and saw the perfect opportunity for one of your "lovely deals".'

'Look, Midget Sherlock,' says Hugo. 'You're making some very serious accusations. Now you might have some beef with Gordon here, but that's nothing to do with me.'

'I can't prove you stole *The Owls of Grey Gardens*, even though I know that you did. But I can prove that you gave a deliberately false valuation of *this* book and then got one of your staff to come and buy it for peanuts so that you could re-sell it, and maybe that's not against the law but it's wrong and deceitful and we're going to tell everyone about it so that no one watches your stupid programme ever again. You're a liar and a thief ... and you wear really stupid hats!'

Taylor waves his mini-cam at Hugo. 'Welcome to *The Real World*!'

Suddenly Max picks up the sound of frantic barking in the distance. She's been preoccupied and only notices now that Fang is nowhere to be seen. 'Fang!' she shouts, and runs through the door in the side of the shop into Smythe Towers, following the sound of the barks. Hugo, Gordon, Tiffany, Taylor and Lori all follow. The corridor stretches a long distance and Max is suddenly scared. She's never heard Fang so frantic before. What if Hugo has guard dogs and they're attacking Fang? She thinks of the kinds of dogs she's seen on telly that are used to hunt foxes. She runs flat out along the corridor through another door and out into a grand hallway. She stands, momentarily dazzled, and then runs to an open door where the barking is loudest. She swings the door wide and finds herself in a library bigger than the public one in New Heath. She pauses a moment to take in the strangeness of a library in the middle of a house. Fang comes scrabbling over to her barking crazily.

'Fang!' she says and tries to hold him but he pulls away, racing back to the same spot next to one of the shelves. She chases after him. He's sniffing furiously at a book on the shelf with a yellow spine.

'*The Owls of Grey Gardens*!' Max reads aloud, just as everyone else catches up. Lori runs to get the book and checks it over – she points out her parents' embossed initials for Taylor to film. She bends down and cautiously reaches out to Fang. She strokes his head softly and he licks her face. 'Clever boy,' she says.

CHAPTER TWENTY

Nan comes in as I'm making tiny adjustments to the furniture in the study.

'That was Max's mum on the phone,' she says.

'Is everything OK?'

'Yes, they've had some good news for a change. One of her work pals is moving in with her boyfriend and needs someone to rent her flat. Apparently, it's much better than where they are now and a bit cheaper too as they'll be renting it direct and not through some agency. Looks like they're moving again and this time they can take Fang with them.'

'Fang's going?' I ask.

'He is.' Nan looks at me. 'How do you feel about that?'

I think for a moment. 'Well ... he is a smart dog. Might even make a good detective dog, but...'

'He is a dog?' suggests Nan.

'Yes.' I nod.

'And he makes you a bit nervous.'

'Well … he's just a bit unpredictable, and he jumps up and I know he wouldn't bite me but his teeth are sharp and … it's possible that I'm a little bit scared of dogs.'

'I know, love. You've done very well. I'm glad we've had him here for a bit just to show you how there's nothing really to be scared of. He's such a lovely boy.'

'Will you miss him, Nan?'

'Maybe a little bit, but I'm glad he's going back home. I think Max needs him more than I do.'

'Besides,' I say.

'Besides what?'

'You've got Mr Meacham to get out and about with now.'

'I suppose so,' says Nan. 'We're thinking of getting the bus and going to the opening of the new Morrisons superstore next week.'

'Fang's really going to miss out,' I say.

'Triple points to the first hundred customers, love. Triple points!'

I look around the study. I'm satisfied that it looks pretty much the same as it does on Mum and Dad's old video now. *The Owls of Grey Gardens* is back in its rightful spot on the shelf with the rest of the Pelikan House series all in the right order.

After Fang found the book, Hugo and Gordon had a massive argument in front of us, each one blaming the other, which only ended when Gordon punched Hugo quite hard and made his nose bleed. Tiffany looked horrified. She told us to take the books and go. Taylor and Mr Probert edited all the footage, along with the bits of video I took at the *Treasure Hunters* Open House and posted the full story on *The Real World*. It took less than an hour for it to spread to all the major news sites. Hugo has been sacked by his TV company and he and Gordon are being questioned by the police. Apparently there have been various 'irregularities' in their business activities. The best bit was the front page of all the newspapers the next day. It was a shot from Taylor's footage: Gordon landing a punch on a red-faced Hugo. Nan has it pinned up on the kitchen wall.

She watches me as I move the two grey armchairs to just the right angle.

'I don't know why it's so important to have it exactly the same,' she says.

'I'm not sure either. It just doesn't feel as if the case is closed properly until everything is back in its right place.' I hesitate for a moment. 'You know, I think I need to watch it one more time just to check we've got it right.' I click on the video file for what might be the hundredth time, but I must tap on the wrong part of the screen, because something pops up that I've never seen before. It's a volume bar.

'Nan!' I shout. 'The player has its own volume setting!'

'What, love?' says Nan, coming over to see.

'It was on mute!' I click on the icon and straightway I hear the background hiss of the recording, morning birdsong, a distant siren and then … my dad's voice.

Dad: Hello, Loretta! Happy 18th birthday! I know you're all big and grown up now, but we thought we'd introduce you to yourself back when you were just a tiny dot.

Mum: Hello, sweetheart. Look! This is how you started out … with your little chubby hands and fluffy hair and funny noises. I suppose you've grown out of those, but right now you're great for sound effects – little snorts and wheezes and sighs and gurgles. I'd like to learn the language. I think the idea is that we're supposed to teach you to speak, but I prefer the other way round.

Dad: So, the plan is to have a big garden party on your 18th birthday. All your friends will be there and all your brothers and sisters, however many of them there are…

Mum: Six! Eight! Let's think big!

Dad: Hmmm … maybe … anyway, just when you're least expecting it, we'll present you with a spade and get you to dig up this weird box that we've buried.

Mum: But … that's only if you grow up to be the kind of person who likes parties … and surprises. If not, we'll be doing something low key and quiet.

Dad: I spent my 18th birthday in Blackpool with my mates. I lost my wallet, then I got sunburned and then a seagull pooed on my head. I hope your day is going a lot better!

Mum: I spent my 18th birthday in New Heath with my mum and then my friends came round later. Mum made an enormous coffee cake – which is my favourite – and wore this crazy hat she'd knitted with 'World's Proudest Mum' on the front.

Dad: Oh dear, I guess you know all about your nan's hats by now.

Mum: It was nice! I mean, she didn't wear it out in the streets – that might have been embarrassing, just around the house. I'm going to make sure I wear exactly the same hat when you're 18 ... which is today! So erm ... I guess I'm wearing the hat right now in real life!

Dad: This is all getting a bit weird.

Mum: Sorry. Time travel is confusing.

Dad: We just want to say Happy Birthday!

Mum: Happy Birthday! We love you.

Dad: We love you! Shall I stop it now?

Mum: Thanks for spending your life with us! Hope we've done an alright job!

Dad: Finished?

Mum: Hope you still like us even when we do embarrassing things like dig up time capsules on your birthday!!

Dad: I'm going to press stop...

Mum: Byeeeeeeeeeee

'Bye,' I say to the screen and then sit staring at the freeze frame.

Nan says nothing for a long time and then she puts her hand on my head gently. 'Come on, love,' she says. 'Let's go out for a walk. Get some fresh air.' Fang comes racing in at the mention of a walk and then the doorbell goes. Nan goes out to answer it.

'It's only Max!' calls Nan. I'm still sitting in front of the laptop when Max comes in. After a while she sits down next to me.

'Lori, are you OK?'

Her voice gives me a shock. 'What? Me? Yes, I'm OK.'

'Oh,' she says slowly, 'I get it. You heard the news about the flat, didn't you? I'm sorry I'm taking Fang back. I know how hard it's going to be.'

'Oh…' I say. 'It's OK. You know me: brave.'

Max smiles with relief. 'You're pretty tough, you know.'

Nan comes in. 'Tough? I'll say so. You both are. Nobody better mess with you pair.'

Max has Fang on his lead. 'Especially not when Fang's with us.'

'Do you like the little coat I've knitted for him?' asks Nan.

'Yeah, it's great. I like the pattern.'

I guess it looks like a pattern from where she's standing. The angle Fang's pointing means Max can't see that Nan has knitted 'Cutie Pie' in big letters all along the side of his coat.

'Come on, girls and boy,' says Nan. 'Let's see what the world has for us today.'

EPILOGUE

Six months later

Ryan
Ryan Johnson was tried and sentenced to five and a half years in prison. He did not cooperate with enquiries and failed to provide information on the wider criminal network of which police believe he is a member and which continues to operate in New Heath.

Calum
Calum Osborne has started at a new school and is doing better with his attendance. He doesn't go to Swingo Park any more.

Hugo Smythe
Hugo Smythe is awaiting trial for conspiracy to defraud. His television and publishing contracts have been terminated and Salvaged Treasures has gone out of business. Hugo is currently selling

off his library of rare books to fund his legal expenses.

Gordon Trent
Gordon Trent is wanted by police on charges of conspiracy to defraud. He has not been seen since assaulting Hugo Smythe at Smythe Towers. The police suspect he has fled overseas on a false passport.

Tiffany Clipboard Woman
No charges have been bought against Tiffany Fortescue-Brown who police believe lacked any awareness of her employer's actions. She now works as an events organiser in Cheshire specialising in luxury weddings.

Taylor
Taylor Barclay won the prestigious Junior Reporter of the Year award for his work on *The Real World* exposé of Hugo Smythe. He and Mr Probert sometimes visit other schools together giving talks about making and posting videos online. Taylor's mum still won't let him have his own key.

Mr Cheetham

Mr Cheetham is currently off school for two weeks with a twisted ankle after stepping on a small rubber ball in the year-five cloakrooms. He is spending his convalescence time plotting the next stage in his ongoing campaign against trip hazards.

Mr Probert

Mr Probert's Friday afternoon news club continues to be very popular. He sometimes uses old shopping channel videos to illustrate certain production techniques to the children. They all agree that his work on the Eternal Sparkles range of cubic zirconia rings was ground-breaking.

Mad Marge

Marjorie Willis recently found her purple windcheater hidden inside another coat in her understairs cupboard. She remembers now that she never actually took it on her visit to Swingo Park. 'They don't call me mad for nothing,' she was reported as saying to Nan.

Max's mum

Angela Ellington applied for and got a promotion

to shift supervisor. She's hoping to study English and Maths GCSE if she ever has a little more time.

Mr Meacham

At Nan's suggestion, Mr Meacham has introduced a loyalty card scheme in his sweet shop and business has picked up. Points are awarded not on quantity but on diversity of the sweets purchased. He has asked Nan to please call him Maurice.

Nan

Nan is still devoted to car boot sales and hunting for valuable vintage and antique items. Last week she sold the rotten-looking rocking horse with a missing leg to just the right buyer for £150 more than she paid for it. She took Lori and Mr Meacham for an early-bird special at the local carvery in celebration.

Max

Max's new maisonette backs onto the Heath Brook Recreation Ground where she's able to catalogue local wildlife and train Fang. She's recently started a Saturday job at Meacham's sweet shop and is saving her earnings for a pair of bird-watching binoculars.

Fang

Fang continues digging holes and chasing smells. He has yet to return a single stick Max has ever thrown.

Lori

Lori has finally redecorated her bedroom. The walls are now white and covered with pinboards and newspaper cuttings on local crimes ... except for one, next to her bed, which remains yellow, covered with rainbows, stars, mythical creatures and a photo of her mum as a little girl.